The Inscrutable Mr. El

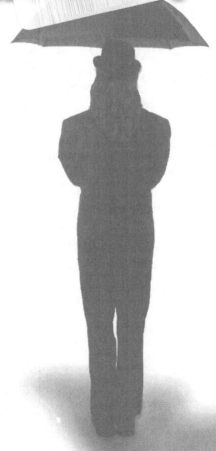

Spinsters Ink

Visit us at www.spinstersink.com

2013

Spinsters Ink
P.O. Box 242
Midway, FL 32343

Editor: Katherine V. Forrest
Cover designer: Sandy Knowles

ISBN: 978-1-935226-58-1

About the Author

Marlene Leach has had fiction and poetry published in *Lavanderia: A Collection of Women, Wash and Words; The Absinthe Literary Review; Southern California Review; Funeral Party; Threshold; Lost Worlds; Mouse Tales Press, Askew, and Black Petals.* She has worked as a freelance journalist for over 15 years, served as a Marine, worked as a nurse and her non-fiction has been published in *Nvestment Magazine, Get Up and Go, Mature Lifestyles, Naples Daily News, Monadnock Ledger, Nantucket Beacon, Salon.com, Union Leader,* and *Ambience Magazine.* She currently lives in Albuquerque, NM where she teaches Intro to Novel Writing at UNM Continuing Education. She is a graduate of NYU Tisch School of the Arts and the Master of Professional Writing Program at University of Southern California. *The Inscrutable Mr. Elizabeth* is her first, but far from her last, novel.

For my parents, who never stopped believing.

CHAPTER ONE

Albuquerque, NM—Present Day

> *Why did you do it? Why did you do it?*
> *That's all they want to know. I did it because I was sick and tired of being a nobody, sick and tired of rented apartments and used cars and a life guaranteed to begin and end in mediocrity. I was sick of people looking at me and never seeing me because there wasn't anything to see. In short, I was sick of everything and maybe I have a bad attitude, that American sense of entitlement that says you're all going to grow up and be rock stars and actresses and millionaires. And then you find out you won't, so you get pissed as hell because you just discovered, like so many before you, that the American dream is a lie. And most people live with that, and they tell themselves it's not quiet desperation that leads to compromise, it's growing up and they try and find beauty in the small things because small things are all they're going to ever have. Fuck that. I want the big things and I want them now because why shouldn't I have them? What makes you better than me? Who thinks*

he can decide whose dreams shall live and whose shall be pushed aside? An asshole. Well, I'm an asshole too. I know that. I have a chip on my shoulder the size of Texas, and it's not going anywhere soon. I'm not sorry for anything. I killed him because he deserved it, and I'd kill him again if given the chance. He was a rapist and had nothing to offer but misery and eating disorders to a new generation of women popping antidepressants to get through the miserable day of being born with a hole that some bastards believe they have a right to invade. Last time a guy raped me I was too young to do anything about it, but I swore I'd kill the next one who ever tried, and I did. Call me what you want, but I ain't a liar. The only thing different I'd do is try not to get caught. Now excuse me, you dumb assholes, because you left the window open so I'm outta here, ha ha ha, see you in the goddamn funny pages.

"That's it," Detective Schmitt said heavily. "That's all she wrote." He ran a hand through his thinning gray hair, mouth creased in a frown. He had a corrected cleft palate and the scar made him resemble an old tomcat that has seen and done too much.

Elizabeth Highsmith studied the paper in silence. It had started out as a plain, two-page, typewritten confession, the details noted dutifully by the stenographer who'd taken the verbal confession, but apparently the details hadn't been accurate enough to suit their suspect because she'd flipped over the paper and written her rant out by hand. Now the second-story window of the courthouse was wide open, curtain flapping in the breeze, and the suspect was long gone. Elizabeth found it noteworthy that the prisoner had signed it with a question mark rather than a name.

When they'd taken her into custody, she'd given her name as Belle Gunness. The name had sounded vaguely familiar, but Elizabeth hadn't been able to place it. Now she did. Belle Gunness, 1859-1908. A Norwegian-born woman who allegedly killed over forty men, mostly husbands and suitors, for their money, and also possibly two of her children. Began her dubious career after attending a dance where a rich man assaulted her and kicked her, causing her to miscarry her first child. The man was never prosecuted due to his station in life.

Elizabeth straightened, placing one hand in the small of her back, and stretching, feeling a bit like a cat as she did. She wondered if Detective Schmitt also believed *she* resembled a cat, a short, stout, stern, little breed with long blond hair and a bit of extra fur. *(I'm not fat, I'm just fluffy.)* "Who put her up here?" she asked.

Detective Schmitt shrugged helplessly. "She refused an attorney, said she wanted to represent herself. Legally, she's allowed access to the courtroom law library. She'd been up here all week, never a bit of trouble..." He trailed off, realizing how he was just digging himself in deeper. Nobody was going to come out of this looking good. Speaking just made it worse.

Elizabeth nodded, keeping her own face carefully blank, inscrutable. For the most part, the police officers she worked with were good, hard-working, competent people. But every now and then they really screwed up and that's when she was called in. To clean up their mistakes and collect their garbage when it escaped their confines. Bounty hunter wasn't listed as a job possibility on most applications and it made tax time a real bitch, but it was still a job, and she was good at it. The best, really. She'd been called in on eight cases since she'd started two years ago, and she'd found every one of the escapees within a month, two at most.

She set the confession back down on the wood table of the library, and leaned against the wall, folding her arms. "So what do we do know about this clown?" she asked.

Detective Schmitt shrugged. "Unfortunately, not too much. We ran her fingerprints and nothing came up so she's not former service and has no priors. Gave her name as Belle Gunness, but had no identification on her. Other than that, no one seems to know much. Here's the physical rendition the police artist did."

He handed over a sketch. Elizabeth studied a depiction of a woman in her early to mid-twenties with short dark hair and dark eyes and a pointy chin. Estimated height and weight was five feet and a hundred pounds.

"Tiny thing," she remarked. "I wonder how she overpowered him?"

The murder itself had been gruesome. She'd already read the details. Throat slit with a knife after an initial stab into the jugular. In the parking lot behind a local bar. The victim had died almost instantly, had been found dead by a couple leaving the bar.

"Can you find her?" Detective Schmitt asked.

Elizabeth shrugged. "No one's gotten away from me yet. I'm guessing you already spoke to the bartender where the victim was found?"

Detective Schmitt nodded. "Yeah. No one remembers seeing her there. Typical. It was Friday night though, and crowded, so who knows?"

Elizabeth nodded though privately she thought that if the girl had been in the bar, someone would have remembered her. She had a distinctive face, rather elfin, and a woman alone in a bar always stood out as Elizabeth well knew. Women alone in bars were usually grouped in one of two categories: those looking to snag a man, and barflies. Sometimes both. If the girl's story was true and the man had tried to attack her, she'd either been passing by the bar or on the way in. Or maybe—and it was a grimmer thought but it had to be considered—perhaps the girl simply waited outside the bar, hoping someone *would* attack her. The whole first part of her rant had a tinge of the narcissistic whining of a serial killer looking for any reason to rationalize what she did rather than admit the truth, which was that she did what she did because she wanted to and because she liked killing. Only later did the rape talk pop up and even a hint that it might have been self-defense. Perhaps that was all "normal." Elizabeth had met plenty of women in prison who liked to wear the bad attitude and play at being hard-asses because it was better to be seen, even by yourself—*especially* by yourself—as a sociopath rather than a victim. Some truths are easier than others to live with.

Elizabeth understood all that because once she hadn't been so different.

New York, NY—2004

Tread slowly and with great caution.

The words leaked up from deep within her subconscious like oil, slowly seeping out and creeping over the landscape of her conscious mind until they finally enveloped all aspects of it, and her body relaxed as it felt the message being received.

Elizabeth didn't get messages that often from such a deep place and when she did, she listened, because they were always right. Usually it was trivial stuff: sometimes a flash of what ponies would win at the track. Not every time, not even most of the time, but often enough that she simply didn't bet unless she saw that faint yellow glow over the numbers of the winning horses. Her winnings kept her in enough money that she didn't have to work. She knew many people wondered how she got her money and how she lived so well even though she never seemed to hold a job. Many wondered but few knew, partly because it amused her to be so cryptic and inscrutable, and because who would believe the truth?

Her talent also sometimes told her what job a person held, whether they were married or single. Whether a team would win or lose. What song was coming on the radio. Sometimes it had been a simple feeling with a single message: *Stay home tonight. Don't go down that street, turn left instead.* Whenever that happened, she listened.

And once or twice there had been other incidents like the man on the subway. She'd been standing by the platform and turned on some instinct, and there he was coming down the stairs. A perfectly average-looking man, and yet she'd felt a sudden wave of rage and hatred toward him, he'd made her sick, and she'd turned away to avoid literally throwing up. She walked away quickly down the platform, and she could feel him following her, and sure enough, when she got in the car, there were only three other people in there, and he'd come in after her and sat down across and at a slight diagonal. They both pretended to be unaware of the other, but five minutes into the ride, he'd unzipped his pants, pulled out his pud and began jerking off. She was nineteen, and hardly shocked by the sight of a man's penis. What bothered her was the malevolence behind it, the fact that he was doing it for the sole purpose of trying to shock and intimidate her.

Fucker.

She'd shoved her hand abruptly into the pocket of the army jacket she always wore as if she were going for a gun and had the pleasure of seeing his hand stop midstroke, and he flinched back for a moment. Just a moment, but she saw it from the corner of her eye and smirked inwardly, keeping her face impassive, inscrutable, revealing nothing. She felt his brief fear then his anger. He had plans for her and had since the moment he'd seen her. She didn't know the particulars of those plans but she had no desire to be a participant.

She got off at the next stop, felt him follow her. She ducked behind a newsstand, and walked around and stepped back on the train. Her predator was clever. Her trick only fooled him for a few seconds, maybe thirty at most, but that was all the time she needed. The doors slid shut and she peered at him through the scratched glass, their eyes finally locking for the first and last time. She felt his rage and frustration, saw his hands clench into fists, and a slow smile spread over her face as her own hand rose up and flipped him the bird just as the train began to pull out. She felt and saw him glaring after her, and then the subway was in the dark tunnel, heading back to Brooklyn, and his presence receded. Another escape.

A finger tapped her on the shoulder as she stood on the subway platform now, remembering that day. A soft voice purred in her ear.

"Elizabeth Highsmith? We'd like to talk to you."

Too late, Elizabeth saw all of them in her mind and knew what they'd come for. In her mind, she saw the wheel of her life shifting, and she tried to push it back, but it was all too late. The wheel would turn, and she would turn with it. There was no choice.

Albuquerque, NM—Present Day

She pushed her thoughts away from her long and complicated past, and thanked Detective Schmitt for the information. Outside in the temperate September air, she studied the sketch of the girl she'd be finding.

Who are you?

Flashes of random images scampered through her mind: cereal puffs eaten from a porcelain bowl on a dingy card table in a kitchen with chipped and dirty linoleum flooring, a car key taped together with medical tape to keep it from falling apart, ratty white sneakers, jagged chewed nails with dirt under them…a life of cheap broken things. And under it all, a current throbbing and running, strong and dark blue, a river of rage and fury that would never run dry. *It's what keeps me going. Love is fleeting but hate is eternal.*

Was it her own thought or the girl's? Sometimes it was hard to tell the difference when she started to crawl into the head of another. But that was all right. She always got out in the end, and that's what mattered.

Sure. Except for those few unpleasant trips to the hospital…

She pushed those thoughts away. It didn't do any good to dwell on unpleasant things, and besides, she had her…talent much more under control now than in those early days. Not that she'd had much choice in the matter. The bastards had worked her over and worked her over until some days her hands were shaking and she'd thrown up even a glass of milk. When drinking herself to sleep became the norm not the exception. Ms. Highsmith, are you familiar with the NSA? Ms. Highsmith, are you familiar with a process known as Controlled Remote Viewing? She hadn't been familiar with either at the beginning, but by now she was all too familiar with both of these things and a lot more besides.

She found it strange that the military had been so interested in her, and it wasn't until years later that she even realized how they'd found her. She'd gone to New York University after high school with no clue of what she wanted from the future so she'd started as a liberal arts major, taking a variety of courses that interested her. One of them had been a class on psychic phenomena and at one point in the class, all the students had been given a battery of tests to rate their psychic or clairvoyant abilities.

They'd not been shown the results which the professor had rounded up at the end of the class and taken home for his own perusal, but Elizabeth had a feeling that she'd done very well. Ever since puberty she'd had a feeling that she was "different" but it was hard to define in what way. She'd simply dismissed it as very keen intuition. It wasn't until a year later, after her parents were killed by a drunk driver, and she'd had a small nervous breakdown that ended with her dropping out of NYU and making a living at the pony track, that she'd started to realize just how different.

So had that nice old bearded Santa Claus figure of a professor been turning over results such as hers to the government? Or was the government the one who'd funded the program in the first place and thus kept their own tabs? Elizabeth supposed it didn't matter. What did matter was that they'd become aware of her, and she had no doubt that it was through the tests she'd been administered in that class. Only after they'd recruited her would she be challenged and trained and really learn how to take her abilities to a whole new level, and the process had been grueling. Isolation chambers, expressionless people who met with her one-on-one and battered at her mind until she learned to put up shields to defend herself, strange drugs injected into her arm to "enhance" her abilities, but mostly isolation except for the trainers, other people with gifts similar to hers and equally inscrutable faces except for the constant fear lurking behind their eyes, but they would never discuss that or anything personal with her. Nobody spoke to her unless it was work-related and this went on for a year and a half until she got her first Controlled Remote Viewing assignment…

Her hands were shaking even now. With some effort, she managed to steady them before she got in her car and drove home to Taylor Ranch. She had her own house, a small but tasteful three-bedroom with a large backyard. It was in a nice suburban area on the west side of town, just behind Petroglyph State Park. So veddy middle class, it amused her, but never too much. New Mexico was a good place to disappear, a place for people who wished to have no past, and she'd chosen it because of her attraction to the arid infinite landscape of the desert that promised enough sand and sun to burn or wear down any baggage from another life.

She was grateful too in a way that only the truly poor could be when given something better, something that wasn't grubby and broken.

My thought or hers.

It was hard to tell. Whoever this girl was, her personality was powerful, punching like a boxer through the fabric of time and space. There was no difficulty honing in on her; the difficulty would be in not being consumed by her while still maintaining close enough contact to eventually determine her identity and whereabouts. That was the hard part because only emanations that resonated emotionally could be shared across the distance of space.

Elizabeth stripped off her suit and all her clothes then got ready for bed, putting on a pair of blue men's pajamas with white stripes, long sleeves and long pants.

I wonder what *she's* wearing tonight, she thought, and for a quick moment she had a flash of a dingy dim room with a radiator and a sink, fire escape, an arm reaching out to adjust the heat, tribal tattoo band around a skinny bicep. Dirty tank top and men's boxers.

Fire escape, Elizabeth thought. So it's a city.

She went back out to her living room. Like the rest of her house it was a study in tidiness and middle-class furnishings, neither too tasteful nor too garish. Merry Maids came once a week.

As for the normalcy of the house, that was an art form Elizabeth studied the way an entomologist studied bugs. Normalcy was largely myth, but it did exist as an ideal if not a reality, and Elizabeth pursued imitating this with the dedication of an Olympic athlete. In this way, she never attracted attention and that was the point, to embody the archetype of normalcy so completely that it generated no interest in her whatsoever from outside parties. Her few quirks she doled out to herself like a miser or a poor child with a box of chocolates, hoarding them then savoring them in the privacy of her own home. Men's pajamas. Perfume rather than cologne but only at home. A collection of Japanese haikus written on grains of rice kept in the bedside drawer. All of these things were her treasures and too much would have been overwhelming. And would do no good for concentration—for her job—if she overdid her distractions. Too much of her mind and how would she occupy anyone else's? She would have filled herself. By leaving empty space, within and without herself, she had room to embody anyone. To become herself was to lose the gift of becoming others. It was a conundrum, and she walked a fine line, but she thought she had mastered the balance quite well. All things considered.

Thus the living room of her house consisted of two Papasan chairs facing the fireplace and in front them a glass-topped wicker coffee table. A large L-shaped brown mahogany desk with a computer on it sat in the corner. Her walls were adorned with several gold-framed Matisse prints. Not her taste, but surely the taste of someone with good refined sensibilities.

Ah, yeah, right. She could feel the identity of her anonymous stranger creeping into the back of her mind, sneering at everything. She hadn't even settled in to focus on this girl, and already she was picking up traces of her, and strong ones. She wondered why that was so. She did *not* like this girl, based on what little she'd read in her screed. It had reeked of the overly pretentious sniveling of a brat with a chip on her shoulder who was willing to justify anything so long as it suited her needs because she really didn't care about the needs of anyone else. If Elizabeth saw anything of her former self there, it did not endear the girl to her in any way; it just made her dislike her even more because she knew damned well she had *not* been a likable teenager or young person and the dislike she engendered had been well-deserved.

She settled into her Papasan chair, legs crossed, closed her eyes and then relaxed her mind with an internal rhythmic thumping sound until her brain waves transformed to the deepest state of sleep, delta brain waves. She could bypass the alpha brain waves because her brain was almost always in a state of alpha now due to meditation and practice. She experienced no anxiety and was incapable of fear. It was part of her disability: such things were deemed necessary for survival. Perhaps, but she was still here, and she didn't miss the crippling anxiety and fear that used to be such a large part of her life before she learned—or was forced to learn—to control her talents.

She focused on the girl in the picture.

Who are you? What is your name?

Immediately she flashed into that dirty room again, but now she could see more clearly. It was dusk, but there were no lights on. A small twin bed in the corner. A sink at the foot of the twin bed. Pea-green cement walls with several cracks running down the cement and no decorations. No TV. Hardwood floor. A bottle of beer resting on the floor beside the bed, and the remainder of a twelve-pack poking out of the sink, on ice. She sensed the girl's presence, knew she was seeing things from her perspective and tried to hone in deeper.

She felt a smug sense of satisfaction undercut on a deeper level by a constant nagging fear which only the beer served to quench for a little while though it would inevitably make things worse in the fear department simply because loss of control was already what this girl was battling and deep down, she knew it. Everything she did was about control, whether it was surrendering all control in a moment of spite because she knew she'd never have perfect control or trying to maintain perfect control above all else.

Name. Name?

Positive or negative, most people had some kind of attachment to their names. It was their identity, after all, and as such, usually very easy for Elizabeth to pick up, the first name at the very least. But not in this case. Elizabeth could see the girl in her head and could see the girl's own self-image which was not at all what she actually looked like although that was common enough; but even in the deeper recesses of her mind, Elizabeth could sense no concrete identity, a name by which this girl was known, and that was unusual and frustrating.

Goddamn it. She lingered in the girl's mind. She could not read thoughts, only impressions and feelings, and most of what she felt was exactly what she would have expected to feel within the mind of a drunk. Self-pity, rage, fear. Occasionally a surprising stretch of contemplation, deteriorating and finally consumed by despair. It was a wonder this one hadn't thrown herself out a window yet. She must be made of tougher stuff than it seemed, at least when she was sober.

Elizabeth gave up and opened her eyes. She had no wish to linger in the mind of a drunk. Her last case had been a drunk as well, a serial killer who preyed on hitchhikers. Elizabeth had only known eight serial killers, but she'd known them more intimately than their own mothers or lovers (if they had them), and she'd noted that all of them had a tendency to abuse substances and seek oblivion or simply a loss of the control they so meticulously maintained at all other times.

Her mind always felt dirty and tired after these hunting expeditions, and after the first four she'd insisted adamantly on being allowed several months to recoup. The time away gave her the chance to inhabit a new mind, a baby preferably or someone small and innocent so that she didn't become too jaded by everything she saw—and essentially became—during the time she was hunting killers. During this off time she made lots of crafts and read children's books, and it was always the nicest period of her life.

Then the call would come. Most of the time it was the New Mexico police precincts or occasionally an out-of-state one. They all knew her. And that was fine. But once in a rare while, even now, it wouldn't be from the police. It would be the Subset, having taken a special interest in a certain killer for reasons of their own, and Elizabeth had no choice but to go. The small rooms and the steady influx of drugs they'd given her during her last year with them when she'd begun to fray and her abilities were diminishing had instilled a respect for them that left no boundary from fear. Essentially, the government still controlled her and if they wanted a killer found, they knew whom to call.

The double click on her phone whenever she made a call attested to the reality that she was still and always would be property of the US Government. She had signed the paper. Of course, she had. She'd been twenty-six with no goals and no prospects other than playing the ponies for eternity, and they'd offered her ten thousand dollars just to sign up, a long list of perks, plus they flattered her incessantly, something to which she'd seldom been subjected before and quite enjoyed. They had told her she would be doing "intelligence work" with her abilities. They had made it all sound quite fun and easy, and assured her over and over that she would be doing good things, helping her country and saving innocent people from "bad guys." By the time she realized there were only four other people on the bus taking her from boot camp to Fort Meade where NSA headquarters was located, and she would begin her training, it was too late. That double-click on the phone was a lifelong companion and fighting it was not even an option. And the Subset was beyond even the NSA in terms of secrets, spying, assassinations, and with a carte blanche to do whatever they saw fit. The laws that governed the rest of the country seemed not to apply to them. It was a small group but very elite with a seemingly unending source of funding and resources.

Why they'd called for this one wasn't entirely clear. Detective Schmitt had called first, and that was not unusual. Elizabeth had considered turning down the case. She'd just completed one three months ago, and it was too soon. Then the Subset had called. There had been something chilling in the very ringing of that call, and Elizabeth had known it was them even before she'd answered. But she was too afraid to not answer the phone. "Yes?" she'd whispered, picking it up. "Mr. Elizabeth? Take the case from Schmitt," a raspy voice ordered. Then there was a click and the dial tone. That was all, but it was enough, and Elizabeth had met with Detective Schmitt the next day. Mr. Elizabeth. At first she had hated that nickname—Mr.

Elizabeth—when they'd started calling her that in training. She never knew who had started it, but it was clearly a mockery of her obvious masculine traits. However, the mockery stopped as her talents grew stronger, and she had grown to like the name and to refer to herself by it.

(Damn right, you can call me Mister and snap to when you do it!)

At first glance, the case seemed like routine manslaughter, but there was obviously more to it, and Elizabeth suspected that like her, the Subset also believed the girl might be a serial killer. There were more female serial killers at work than most people suspected; they just didn't get caught as often as men, not because they were always more clever though in some cases that was true, but simply because most people didn't believe a woman was capable of such acts. At best, a woman might get caught for one homicide, but never more than that so the list of women serial killers was disproportionately low when compared to the actual number—as Elizabeth well knew. Aileen Wuornos had been caught, but only after getting away with far more than anyone with a borderline IQ and a substance abuse problem warranted.

Elizabeth wondered what political affiliations the girl had, if any. The Subset usually didn't get involved in serial murder unless the suspect had been spouting heresies politically, even if it was just drunk mouthing off of political threats against the powers that be on an online message board. And even then, they usually left that for the regular NSA boys. Twice, the Subset had called her to find and apprehend a wanted fugitive, and Elizabeth had not known either time why exactly she'd truly been called. She knew it was not the killing. The Subset did not care about murder. That was routine and irrelevant for them. There was some reason they were interested in this girl. Damned if she knew what it was, though.

* * *

L. was getting drunk and listening to Peter Gabriel. "Family Snapshot," one of her favorites, but she paid it no mind now, lost in the murkiness of her own thoughts. *Who lies behind my sleeping eyes?* She giggled, but it was no laughing matter. Someone had been rummaging in her mind. She knew. Oh yes. You can't kid a kidder. Fucking bastards. Probably the government. She knew all they were up to and none of it was good. Old Ted Kaczynski had the right idea; he just didn't think on a broad enough scale. A few mail bombs weren't going to get anyone's attention these days of raining blood and daily baths of mass murder. You needed to be ambitious. Blowing up the Senate while it was in session—now there was a dream that had meat. You could sink your teeth into that one and chew on it for a while, and the taste was sweet and tender like a fine brisket. Your name would be in every history book for a thousand years if you succeeded. Maybe you'd even get a holiday like Guy Fawkes. Better to burn in infamy than die in obscurity. Still, one thing at a time.

She closed her eyes, setting her beer bottle on the floor beside the bed by feel, careful even in her drunkenness not to spill a drop, and behind her eyes there was a great burning taking place. It would start in the cities and work its way out, a purification of the masses where everything would be washed clean and the world could start again. For a long time, she'd believed she didn't matter until she realized that was a subjective view. Matter to what? The course of history? If posterity was to be the judge, then all you needed to do was simply take up the pen and write your own destiny. If you were lucky, it was given unto you to build and create. But if not, then you could tear down all that was rotten. To everything and everyone, a time and place. There was so much wrong that could be fixed… erased…changed. So much to do and so little time. At least she still had a little money from the last scumbag she'd killed. If she was very frugal, and she usually was, it could last another two months. And in the meantime, she'd research…scour the sex offender registry online…start scouting prospects out…

She felt herself dropping into sleep and for just a moment, she saw an image of a rather severe-looking blond woman sitting in a suburban house. In the house, but not of it. No, clearly not that. Who are you? she wondered.

The song was set on repeat on her CD player and had started again, looping over and over, but she never got tired of it. The last thought she had before she fell asleep, and the song had drifted out of her head:

I am nobody.

Somebody would have to die.

CHAPTER TWO

Elizabeth woke up in the morning her head hurting and her mouth dry as if she'd been drinking heavily the night before, though she seldom drank and wasn't a heavy drinker when she did.

Not anymore, but that wasn't always true, was it, my little dark one?

"Shut up," she said aloud. She was used to the voices in her head, the constant conversation and knew they weren't real, just facets of her own mind speaking to her, but it didn't make them any less annoying for all that.

The sun was shining in through the slats; it was a nice day in Albuquerque. It seldom rained here. Despite that, Elizabeth could already feel that it was going to be a bad day. The best thing to do was stay in the house. Not even get dressed. There were a lot of days like that for her. She wasn't afraid of going out so she didn't view herself as agoraphobic; she just really really liked it in her house. At least that was the lie she was telling herself this month. She'd found it easy to do. You could tell yourself anything and know it was a lie, but if you said it often enough, you began to believe it and in time, it would *become* the truth.

She lay in bed for a while, her eyes closed, enjoying the safety of the bed, the knowledge that no one could hurt her, the loaded gun on her bedside table always within reach, ensuring that this would stay a safe place. She was incapable of fear and did not view sleeping with a gun at arm's reach as unusual: it was just prudent.

God created woman; Smith and Wesson made us equal.

Eventually she got up and went out to the living room to check her e-mail and see what was happening online. She had a few interactive Scrabble and chess games going on there that she was eager to get back to.

In the living room, she sat cross-legged in her chair at the desk, sipping her morning coffee and surfing the net for a while, playing games and reading the news. It was very peaceful. She was not shirking her duty to find the killer. It was just easier to relax, clear out her mind that way, and then pursue the killer when her mind was calm and unobstructed. For some reason, she had snatches of Peter Gabriel songs in her head. She liked Peter Gabriel well enough, but he wasn't anyone she listened to regularly so she had no idea why the songs were there. Still, she was used to random flotsam in her head (all frequencies were received on *her* station) so she didn't think anything of it.

Je suis sans frontieres.

The day passed quietly as Elizabeth kept her mind unfettered and free, but there were no traces or impressions of the girl. That wasn't unusual. If her target was especially calm or sleeping, Elizabeth could lose all sense of where he or she was, and after the residual hangover she'd experienced this morning, she wouldn't be surprised if her quarry slept all day.

I will find you, she thought. There was no smugness or even threat in the thought just a matter-of-factness borne from experience. In the meantime, as her target had given her no name, not even a first name, she would have to assign something.

L., she thought abruptly. The letter popped into her head

from nowhere, and it seemed oddly appropriate. Elizabeth wondered if she'd stumbled onto the first letter of the girl's name. It was possible. In the meantime the girl would be L. and at least an identity, even an assigned one, would help Elizabeth focus on her and find her. A concrete identity was crucial in the discovery process. Without it, the girl could be anyone, anywhere.

Identity is everything, Elizabeth thought, and the realization left her strangely bothered and disturbed.

She tried to focus. That day and the next. And the day after that. September slipped into October and then November. The girl seemed to have vanished into the ether of nothingness. Elizabeth received no impressions over these months other than a few random drunken ones, much as she had the first night. She was no closer to figuring out who or where the girl was except that she lived somewhere in the north because it was getting dark earlier there and once there had been a few flurries of snow. That really didn't help much at all. Up north encompassed a large area.

And then the girl went out to kill again.

* * *

She'd hot-wired a car earlier, and now she sat outside The Lion's Paw, a small bar in New Jersey. Her target was Mark Ahern, a sex offender convicted of the rape of an eight-year-old girl. He'd served four months. That was deemed justice. L. knew most people got enraged over things like that, but she didn't. Instead she did something about it. Made her own justice. Rage was a trait only of the impotent. Those who were movers and shakers acted and never felt helpless because they knew they could deal with whatever came up. She had a Bowie knife inside her jacket that she'd bought at an Army-Navy store in Queens. She'd throw the weapon into the Hudson River tonight when she was done. And it would be tonight. It had to be. She'd found Mark six weeks ago and had been watching him ever since. She knew where he lived, where he worked, where he hung out. She also knew that he'd begun seeing a woman two weeks ago. A woman with a ten-year-old daughter.

Oh you bastard.

But that was all right because now she would be a bigger bastard. If you were an asshole, may as well use that trait for good, right? She giggled in the darkness and her breath made small clouds in the darkness of the car. Even with her jacket and gloves on the night was cold, but the heater in the car, an old '77 Chevy Impala, was out of order so she was stuck with it. A very faint sprinkling of snow had begun about an hour ago, and the wind made the snow swirl and dance in the air, pinging against people and cars like bullets as it fell.

And of course it was logical to wait and watch. Make sure you didn't get caught the way she had in Albuquerque. That had been unexpected, a confluence of bad luck. She had been waiting outside the bar for a target, another pedophile, and had been herself attacked. Only the fact that she'd had her knife at the ready had saved her. A bit of irony. The hunter is the hunted, and the world is full of perverts. After she had stabbed him, she'd hoofed it down the road and had a police car not come along, she probably would have gotten away with it. As it was, he'd slowed up to see what she was "up to," and she'd still had the bloody knife in her hand. She never left the knives behind even though she always wore gloves. Better to address all potential outcomes and leave as little for the police to work with as possible. She explained that she'd been attacked, but when asked why she was carrying a knife, she'd only been able to offer up self-defense. Fortunately, they'd seemed to believe her, likely because she was a woman, and what woman didn't need self-defense? What they wouldn't believe was that since she'd just walked away, that she didn't know the attacker. Her escape from the police was dumb luck, and she owed it to even more good luck that she'd made it out of town. She'd hot-wired a car, and drove up to Oklahoma before the car finally died on her, and from there, she'd been able to hitch back to New York. As a woman, you could always get a ride hitching, though if you were squeamish about sex or blow jobs it was probably best not to hitch. L. wasn't squeamish. She'd given enough against her will that she didn't mind doing it so long as she at least got something from the deal. Better than giving it away for free or worse, having it taken by force. And they *would* get it, one way or the other, they always did, so...best to at least name your price and maintain control that way.

However, if she was honest about it, deep down, there was more to these last six weeks than just prudence. The stalking was...fun. The anticipation, the building up of it inside. Knowing that soon there would be release but not too soon. Wait for it. Wait for it...it was better than Christmas. Carving up her kill like a Christmas roast was her Chrissie pressie to herself, and they deserved it so it was good. She was like a dark superhero, fighting crime and ridding the streets of scum. It was a public service, and sometimes she thought if the public knew what she did, they'd put her on the payroll. At least they should.

"I'm a goddamn public servant," she muttered and laughed. She felt high even though she didn't do drugs beyond the occasional joint, and really, being high was no comparison because this was better than being high or even drunk. Her senses felt sharpened, colors seemed brighter.

"I feel so alive...for the very first time," she sang. It was a line from a song, she couldn't remember which, but that was okay. Tonight she was in a happy mood, and everything was good. Tonight she'd get back.

Get back? At what? Who?

She didn't answer. Her mind often asked her questions about things she preferred not to think on, and she was used to ignoring it.

The bar door opened and L. straightened, but it wasn't Mark. She relaxed back in her seat, cracked the window a little and lit a cigarette. It was dark enough, and she was short enough that she was barely noticeable in the car, especially if she slouched as she was doing now. Another hour passed. It was one-thirty in the morning, but she wasn't tired. At two-thirty a.m., Mark finally came out. He was alone. L. waited as he headed over to his car, and then she got out of her own car, unzipping her jacket so she could reach the knife in the specially made pocket she'd sewn in there. His car was only a few cars away from hers. He was weaving slightly as he got his keys out of his pocket. He took in L.'s five-foot-tall female presence and his eyes swept right over her, dismissing her, not seeing a threat or even seeing her. L. smiled to herself. Sometimes your weakness could be used as a strength. If you were clever.

"Excuse me," she said as he reached the door of his car. He paused and turned. L. kept approaching him, speaking as she did. "I was wondering if you had any jumper cables?" she asked, and now she was right next to him, looking up.

He shook his head. "Nah, man. Sorry." He started to turn away.

"I can give you money," L. said, reaching in her jacket, and he turned back, and then there was the slashing of the blade up and over because the throat was surprisingly tough to cut, like sawing through gristle, but she was good at what she did, and she'd had practice. This one went perfect, the blood shooting straight over her head as it squirted out, and she ducked back as he fell to his knees, her eyes darting to and fro for any witnesses, then she pushed him down, straddled him, and slit the throat from one end to the other. Leapt up and hurried back to her car, heart thumping, wishing, just wishing, that there was time to savor this one. It was rare when she could do a kill in the victim's home (*Victim? Ha! They created victims!*) and unless she was somewhere off the streets she didn't dare linger, but she had a wide loopy grin on her face as she got back in her car and her knees were shaking. Her legs felt all rubbery and weak, and she sank back in the seat gratefully, set the knife on the floor of the passenger side, and drove off.

She turned on the radio and it was heavy metal, and she sang along as she drove away, wanting to scream at the heavens, to say ha, fuck you, you think our destiny is written in the stars? I make my own destiny. I am not a god, I AM God! She was laughing aloud now, too hard to keep singing, the thrill of it all coursing through her, better than any orgasm, better than anything, anything at all. To be so powerful...no one could take it from you, and no one unless they'd been there and done what she had done could know what such a victory felt like. A boxer might understand, the pitting of yourself against another and the ensuing victory, but that was as close to an analogy as she could find. In this moment, she felt all-powerful as if she'd never tasted defeat in her life. She felt like a winner.

* * *

The Hudson. New Jersey. Elizabeth woke up on the floor of her living room, gasping but remembering that much, though for a few horrible moments she had no idea who or where she was, what time it was or even what year it was. Her heart gave a few gallops in terror, and then it all slowly came back, and her heart resumed its normal thumping. She picked herself up off the floor gingerly, moving over to her office chair. She'd been in the Papasan chair, and she'd blacked out or had a seizure—she was never sure what happened when she went away like this and the few times it'd happened in public some people said she seized and others said she blacked out. Either way, it didn't matter. She didn't go out often and it was rare enough that this happened. She'd seen everything through L.'s eyes, felt it with her. Done it with her.

And had a part of her *liked* it? Was that why it disturbed her so much to go into the minds of these people because deep down a part of her enjoyed feeling what they felt during those moments? Maybe that's why it was so easy for her to access them. The dark in them spoke to the dark in her. Either way, she always felt guilt when she returned, and it wasn't residual guilt because none of her perpetrators ever felt guilt, certainly not while they were doing it. A couple of them had expressed an intellectual guilt that manifested in a vague form of discomfort after the fact, but that had been rare and not very powerful. The guilt comforted her in an odd way because it proved to her that there *was* a difference between her and the killers with whom she so easily forged a connection.

Even if it was only one thing, sometimes her own guilt was enough to establish the difference between being a killer and merely connecting to one.

Her head hurt and her stomach was churning. She ran to the bathroom and made it just in time to throw up. Her skin felt cold and clammy and several sizes too small. She lay sprawled over the toilet for a few minutes, too weak to move, and then managed to drag herself into the bedroom, pulling off her pajamas as she went. It was too hot, just too damn hot. She touched her belly and wasn't surprised to find it was drenched with sweat. She flopped on the bed facedown just before she would have fallen.

At times like these, it would be nice not to be alone. She knew she must be alone, had to be alone, being what she was, and she was remarkably self-sufficient... But sometimes...

She imagined Darcy was here. Darcy would have gotten her a cold washcloth, massaged her back. Taken care of her simply so she didn't have to do it for herself *all* the fucking time. To be so alone. Darcy. She hadn't thought of Darcy in a long time, but the memory still brought a smile to her face.

New York, NY—1997

The bar was loud and crowded with flashing strobe lights that were clearly meant to cause seizures. She sat gamely on a barstool, wearing her smile like a scar, and blinking because her vision kept blurring, and she wasn't going to cry, wasn't going to cry... This was all so fucking stupid. She never should have come. Did girls always have to travel in pairs? And packs? Jesus, she didn't know who was hooked up with who so how to approach anyone? As far as she could tell, every damn girl in the Bronx had a date tonight except her.

She'd been working up the nerve to come here for weeks: The Beaver Tail. She'd even dressed for it, duded herself up in jeans, black boots, a white button-down shirt and her pride and joy, her black leather motorcycle jacket with the zippers. She'd slicked back her short hair with Brylcreem and at home, looking at herself in the mirror, she'd preened and strutted, imagining herself as quite the stud. Now the Brylcreem just felt sticky, and her jeans probably made her look fat. This whole thing was a bad idea. Still…she wasn't going to go home without at least trying.

She saw a girl near the edge of the bar who was just her type, talking to two other girls. She had short dark hair that accented her feminine features, ripped jeans, a pink tank top revealing a tattoo on her arm. Soft butch and hot as hell. Elizabeth took a quick swig from her bottle of beer, then slid off the barstool and made the long walk down the bar toward the goddess. She tapped her on the shoulder. The girl turned with a quizzical look, one raised eyebrow. She was even more perfect up close.

"Do you wanna dance?" Elizabeth asked, slurring her words in her nervousness. The girl didn't even take time to think about it, just flicked her eyes up and down Elizabeth in a cursory manner then shook her head.

"No thank you." She turned back to her friends.

Elizabeth headed back to her barstool. The walk down to ask the girl had been long, but not nearly so long as the walk back, and her vision was very blurry now. She finally made it to her stool, sat down, wiped her eyes angrily with the back of her hand and took a large defiant slug of beer.

Fuck women. Fuck them all. This was a mistake. She decided to finish her beer and get the hell out of here. If she hurried, she'd still have time to grab a twelve-pack at the Korean deli on the way home before they stopped selling for the night.

"The old shoot down, huh?"

Elizabeth looked up. The speaker was a woman sitting catty-corner from her at the bar, wearing a tux with the top few buttons of the shirt undone. She had dark hair slicked back except for two pieces on either side of her face that she'd pulled down like sideburns just in front of her ears. She looked about forty, maybe a few years older.

It's Cary Grant, Elizabeth thought drunkenly and smiled. Then the woman's words registered and she stared at the condensation on her bottle as it sat on the bar and mumbled "Yeah."

"First-timer?"

Elizabeth nodded, looking up again. She was so grateful to have somebody to talk to in this place that if she had been a more demonstrative person, she would have leapt on this woman, thrown her arms and legs about her and then sobbed and sniveled into her tux, probably leaving a puddle of snot and tears. "How can you tell?" she asked, forcing a smile to her face. She didn't feel like smiling, but she didn't want to drive this woman off either. She wasn't interested in her romantically; she just wanted somebody to talk to in this strange new world, and so far, this was the first sign of any welcome or acknowledgment she'd received.

The lady took a sip of her own drink, what looked like a martini, shaken not stirred, and smiled a little. "I've had nothing better to do for the past half hour but watch you, and your moves are all wrong. You showed up thinking that pretty face of yours would carry you through because that's the way it works with the boys. Then when it doesn't, you approach one girl but with no finesse as if you wanted to take her to the corner for a hot dog in exchange for a tumble. She shoots you down so you come back to finish getting drunk. Is that a fairly accurate description of the night so far?"

Elizabeth laughed in spite of herself. "That pretty much sums it up."

The lady finished her drink and raised one hand imperiously until the bartender caught her eye. She made a swirling motion with her finger while pointing down at the glass. The bartender nodded and disappeared to make her another drink.

"What's your name?" the woman asked. "I'm Darcy. Darcy Wilde. As in Oscar not an animal, but I can be both."

Elizabeth laughed. "Elizabeth. Just Elizabeth."

"It's nice to meet you, Just Elizabeth. Do you want to know what your real trouble is?"

Well, why not? Elizabeth had no clue what she was doing. Any advice was welcome. She nodded.

"You don't like women," Darcy announced.

Elizabeth was startled. This wasn't what she'd been expecting to hear. "I wouldn't be here if I didn't like women," she pointed out, feeling that she was stating the obvious.

The other woman just shook her head. "Nope. You want women and you resent that need especially since they don't want you so deep down you have the whole love/hate thing going on. You're a misogynist, little boy."

Her drink arrived and she stopped pontificating long enough to pick it up and take a deep swallow before continuing.

"Now if you'll take it from an old queen like me, I can teach you how to be a gentleman instead of a punk and succeed with the ladies."

"I thought only men were queens," Elizabeth said.

"Honey, I'm whatever I want to be, and trust me, I'm a queen," Darcy said, flipping her wrist in an exaggerated motion. "I defy all standard notions of gender."

Elizabeth laughed and felt some of her tension leave her. A lot actually. It had been said. It was out in the open. Darcy had even called her little boy. She'd known her at once for what she really was. A girl who often wanted to be a boy. It was a relief to finally be seen and really feel like someone was seeing *you*. She drained the rest of her drink and nodded to the bartender. "You want another?" she asked, noticing Darcy's glass was already empty.

"Darling, I always want another," Darcy said.

"One more for her, and another Dos Equis for me," she said to the bartender.

"You're a man after my own heart," Darcy said.

Elizabeth smiled, the first real smile she'd had in years. "Likewise."

They drank and talked and drank some more. The next thing she knew, she was back at Darcy's apartment, a surprisingly tasteful loft on the upper West Side. Elizabeth tried to keep her cool as if she was accustomed to being surrounded by such beauty, but something must have shown on her face because Darcy smiled a little.

"The advantages to being a gentleman and getting your money the old-fashioned way," she said.

"What did you do?" Elizabeth asked, curious as to what kind of job this strange, intelligent, but drunken person would ever do.

"Inherited it," Darcy said. "I don't *do* work, honey." They both laughed.

Then they were in the living room, sitting on the couch, drinking more, and Elizabeth confided one of her deepest secrets, one of the reasons she'd been convinced for years that she couldn't really like girls even though all her crushes in high school had been girls. Unattainable cheerleader girls who had rounded handwriting and snapped their gum, but still looked so beautiful...

"I just have no desire to, you know—go down there."

Darcy laughed and poured herself another martini. "Sweetie, do you think every straight person performs fellatio or likes it?"

Elizabeth laughed and suddenly her doubts and her big dark secret didn't seem nearly so big or so worrisome. Darcy continued on, nice and wound up now.

"Despite nicknames like muff-diver and carpet muncher, there are plenty of other things two women can do in the bedroom."

"Like what?" Elizabeth asked, thankfully drunk enough to not be shy so she could finally ask the questions that had been bothering her since she was in high school and realized she liked women but had no idea what to *do* with them physically.

"Come with me," Darcy said, standing and swaying just a little.

Elizabeth followed her back to her bedroom where Darcy opened the sliding door of her closet and pulled out a box of toys. "Toys," she said, delight evident in her voice. "Where commerce makes up for what nature forgot!"

Elizabeth laughed and dropped to her knees beside Darcy, and they both peered into the box and began rummaging around. Darcy had a nice collection: vibrators, dildos, Benwa balls, butt plugs, riding crops, bondage gear…you name it, it was in there. Elizabeth laughed with delight.

"How do you use this?" she asked, holding one up.

Darcy smiled. "If I wasn't so drunk, you could almost make me blush." She took the toy away and explained in great detail how it worked. Elizabeth, who now realized she'd been going about everything entirely wrong, listened with her mouth hanging slightly open.

"Amazing, huh?" Darcy said.

"Amazing," Elizabeth agreed. She was feeling very horny and eager to try this stuff out. She stood up and staggered over to the bed and lay down on her back. "Let's try it out," she suggested.

Darcy laughed, came over and removed Elizabeth's boots. "Get under the blankets," she said.

Elizabeth crawled around and finally made her way under the blankets then smiled up expectantly. Darcy looked like the most handsome thing ever to her.

"Queen Elizabeth," Darcy said. "You are a beautiful piece of work, and I am very drunk, but I am still a gentleman, and a gentleman never takes advantage on a first date. Now go to sleep." She bent down and kissed Elizabeth on the forehead.

Elizabeth felt a little disappointed but touched at the same time. "Thank you," she said.

"Not a problem," Darcy said, heading back over to the door. "Sleep tight, little one."

Darcy flipped off the light and softly shut the door behind her. Elizabeth snuggled down in the blankets, burrowed her head into the pillow and passed out immediately.

* * *

Albuquerque, NM—Present Day

That had been Darcy. Elizabeth had continued to see her, and eventually they *had* slept together, each taking turns being on top and with the aid of certain toys, it had been delightful, and Elizabeth had realized she wasn't asexual or frigid, just different. She smiled now just recalling it. It was with Darcy that she had finally embraced being a woman but on her own terms, not what she saw depicted on TV. Embracing her masculine side and realizing she was allowed to have it and not have to be a male had ironically made her less churlish about being a woman: it was for Darcy that she'd grown her hair long, and she'd never cut it since. Embracing feminine things didn't make you weak. Only allowing other people to dictate who you could or could not be made you weak. Elizabeth had gradually realized she didn't *really* want to be a guy; she just wanted to exist on her terms, and with Darcy, she was allowed to do that and she blossomed with the freedom, accepting herself as her own type of lesbian, not a stereotype but a whole person, one facet of which was that she preferred to date and sleep with women.

Darcy's bad habits had finally caught up with her though, and she'd succumbed to a heart attack at age forty-eight. It had been quick and hopefully painless. She'd died almost instantly. Elizabeth had been heartbroken and ended up spending several days in the hospital on suicide watch. Eventually though she realized it was the way Darcy would have wanted it. Darcy had even stated numerous times that she would die before she ever got old, and it would be a heart attack, quick and painless. Elizabeth just missed her. A lot. There had been no one else serious since then.

Still, Darcy *had* taught her how to be a gentleman…and a lady. To run the whole fluid gamut of human sexuality and not limit or define herself according to others' expectations. They'd gone to operas and theatre, traveled to Europe, all things Elizabeth had never done before and which delighted her. She, in turn, had introduced Darcy to her own loves: race tracks, casinos, baseball games, and Darcy had been equally delighted.

Elizabeth's heart had slowed down now, and she no longer felt as sick over the killing she had viewed. She drifted off to sleep, imagining Darcy's strong hands massaging her back—

much of their relationship had consisted of mutual tenderness rather than sex—fully aware that tomorrow or the next day, whenever she felt better, she would be heading to New York to find her target. The Hudson was the key. The girl's thought that she would throw the knife in the Hudson had indicated a return to New York City, and there could only be one reason for returning there. She lived there.

Elizabeth had vowed never to return to New York City. She did not have happy memories of it, and she did not like the place. But, like it or not, fate was hauling her back there anyway. Everything seemed to be going in a perfect circle regardless of her wishes, and she felt like a pawn being moved by some force that she could just dimly sense but not yet see. Not quite.

Who are you?

As always…no answer. Only the screaming of the silence. And behind it the humming of some great machine which Elizabeth could just dimly picture, purring away in a mythical basement, throbbing, humming forever and ever as it went about some dark undefined business.

New York, NY—Present Day

The death bag perched over New York, devouring it slowly, obscuring the edges of the buildings till they bled into something undefined. Elizabeth could see the sickly yellow-brownish pallor of it all from the window of her plane as it headed into LaGuardia. New York was such a teeming place, unhappy and filthy. She knew that wasn't entirely fair; dreams were coming true in this city also, people were falling in love. But you couldn't put this many people together in one place and not have a fair share of misery, and being the way she was, she couldn't help picking up on all of it. It made the city her least favorite place on earth. She gritted her teeth, wishing there were time to order one more screwdriver, but they'd already begun their descent and besides, there was no time for that nonsense today.

Somewhere in this city, L. occupied her own miserable hole, a place of black-and-whites, where justice was harsh but easy and good and evil were drawn with two simple Crayola lines, the boundaries beginning and ending as L. saw fit.

Oh, I know why they think you're dangerous.

Elizabeth was beginning to get a greater sense of why she'd been called in for this girl. The Subset—her division at the NSA, a sub-branch of a sub-branch, accountable to no one—only took interest in certain people who hid in permanent obscurity. The men behind the Subset wore gray and always spoke softly and when they made phone calls, things got done. Always. There were other branches that watched over the more well-known and public figures, but the Subset dealt with the underground and always had. L. was important to them for some reason, and Elizabeth, resenting the feeling of the great machine moving her through more and more difficult paces, yet again couldn't help but wonder why.

The plane touched down with a gentle bump, and the day was cold but sunny, and Elizabeth could no longer see the death bag, but she knew it was there. How long could you live in such a place and not to be touched by it, she wondered. She guessed it wasn't very long. Unconsciously, she'd braced herself in her seat, tensing up as if expecting a blow. It was the way she always approached the cities.

Hunting time.

She disembarked, taking with her only a small carry-on bag. There was no time for baggage claim or any of that nonsense.

Hurry hurry hurry.

Elizabeth wondered from what or whom the urgency came. Another like herself? Or something else, something in the Basement of the Subset where only those with the highest clearance were allowed? Once she too had been to the Basement. Only once. Very few went more than once, and then for one and all the nightmares began, the slow unraveling, and the eventual washout on full disability after certain shock treatments, rubber block in your mouth so you don't bite your tongue, and your brain singed and burned to discredit you forever and wash away the clarity of those memories. A precaution but also a kind of gift.

She made her way through the crowds of the airport and stepped outside into the brisk air. She paused, setting her bag down to button her army jacket. Yes, she'd taken it out of the closet, for this was a call of duty, old business, and it was only fitting. She had just finished buttoning it when a small man, about five feet tall, with olive skin and dark hair slicked over a bald spot, approached her. He was round and had a pleasant face and a soft voice.

"Mr. Elizabeth?"

Only the Subset ever called her that. It was one thing to hear them on the phone; another, to be trapped in their wire mesh spiderweb in person. Shocked, she picked up her bag even as her face paled. He took her by the arm gently, as if she were an invalid, a lover. "Please come this way."

They headed toward a nondescript black Town Car and Elizabeth said nothing for there was nothing to say. She was back in business, the old business, the great machine still churning even now and always able to use her.

* * *

Somewhere in a Basement room a single lightbulb hung from the ceiling by a wire, swinging slightly. The walls were concrete and damp, seeming to exude the very essence of chilliness. The floor was a pea-green with random cracks throughout. A single table with a dingy white top was in the center of the room. A cliché but no less effective at inducing terror. The universal terror it induced was a deliberate choice. It was effective not in spite of being a cliché but because it was a cliché. Elizabeth sat at the table in an uncomfortable metal folding chair, her body perfectly relaxed, her face slack. In the corner, in the shadows, his face obscured, a man in a black suit stood at ease, talking, his hands folded in front of him like a fig leaf. He talked and Elizabeth said nothing.

When she had slid into the car, a man with buck teeth, already in the backseat, had injected her with something, and now her mind floated somewhere on the wall behind her, far out of reach, taking orders and answering questions in a toneless voice. She was aware of her surroundings, but she could not feel her own body and her words came out with no volition in response to certain questions.

It went on for just under an hour. She was given orders and they were hypnotized into her to obey though she would not remember what those orders were later. Then they took her away again. Back out to the waiting car. They drove her through a series of winding streets. She did not know where she'd been but gradually she began to recognize her surroundings and feel returned to her body as the strange far away feeling left her, and the car finally stopped on Mott Street.

"Have a nice day," the driver said, the olive skinned man who had initially picked her up.

Elizabeth did not ask him how he knew she'd been planning to stay on Mott Street. There was a hostel there, but she'd not booked reservations or even told anyone of her plans. It didn't matter. The Subset had its ways. There were others like Elizabeth out there and far better at what she did than she was.

She stepped out of the car, blinking in the sudden sunlight on the sidewalk, as the car slowly pulled away and disappeared down the street like a bad dream. Her head still felt furry and not quite right though she tried to shake it off.

Time to get busy.

CHAPTER THREE

Her thoughts exploded into brilliant and strange patterns like fractals, popping so fast she could not keep up with them. There was no going back. She crouched in the window, keeping her breathing slow and steady, the chair hard under her bottom, but not shifting. Her pulse was even, regulated, everything under perfect control here. The hardest part was keeping her hands from trembling. The air itself seemed to be holding its breath. The world looked alive, relevant through the scope of the rifle in a way that it never did through the normal lenses of the eyes.

And there he was, the man of the hour, coming down the street. His car was in the middle. Breathe, exhale then squeeze, but don't jerk the trigger. Waiting with bated breath for this moment, any moment now it will be, and you've waited your whole life for this moment, everything coming together like the delicate silken strings of a spider web, intricate and interlocking. In a moment you will step into the sunlight out of the darkness of obscurity and into the bright pages of history, into relevance and meaning. Your favorite books, your favorite foods, the car you drove...all of it will be pored over intently later by people trying to understand "why," never understanding that their perusal after the fact is the very reason why, the need to matter, for here the future shapes the past, the possible future, the glorious future, for infamy and fame are gray and walk down the street with interlocked arms, as intimate as lovers and now indistinguishable to anyone with a video camera who just seeks an audience.

Hold your breath. Now breathe…and let the bullet fly. Again. Again.

The world goes still, slips into slow motion. Every shot is true, every shot is real and a bullet hits home, his body jerking to the side, head exploding. Every moment is real, your wide smile undeniable and at last you breathe again, set the gun down and slump to the ground, back against the wall below the window. There is nothing left. It is all over. The screams, the horns blowing, the thundering of feet in the hallway…all of that is irrelevant and far away. It is done, not to be undone. Now you finally know who and what you are, you have sculpted an identity that will live on in chiseled unyielding marble.

Assassin.

Elizabeth jerked awake, drenched in sweat. The room was very still, foreign and unfamiliar and dark.

Who am I? Was it my dream or hers? And do they wish me to stop it…or to do it?

But for that…there was no answer.

She lay in the dark, staring at the fire escape out the window, faintly lit by some far away streetlamp. In the distance, she could hear the white noise of the never-ending traffic and the cry of a distant siren. She found herself craving a cigarette.

But you don't smoke. Not anymore.

No. But she did. L. That bitch. Elizabeth felt a wave of fury rushing over and through her, fists clenched, fingernails digging into her palms. That bitch who'd invaded her head, and it didn't matter that she'd sought L. out, the closer she got, it always felt like this once the hunt was underway. Things became blurry, her personality slowly being leached out like a clumsy artist erasing the pencil outline of something unclear, and the rage filled her, a voice deep within insensate with fury at being obliterated.

She reached over to the cheap blond wood table and flicked on the light. The faint sickly yellow glow left more shadows and darkness in the corners than it lit. The urge for a cigarette was still with her. She sat up on the edge of the bed, gathering her bearings, then reached down and grabbed her jeans and pulled them on over her boxers. Her T-shirt, then her army field jacket. Handcuffs already in the pocket. Opened up her night table drawer, removed the gun from on top of the Bible and tucked it in the back waistband of her jeans. Scooped up the room key and left, not bothering to turn off the light.

Where was she going? Didn't know, just knew that it was time.

Tonight.

She made her way along the narrow corridor of the hallway, the faded red carpet, past the communal bathrooms, then down the winding staircase to the lobby. The night clerk was still awake, sitting behind the bulletproof glass of the reception area, watching TV, and he flicked a brief bored seen-it-all New Yorker's glance her way then went back to the TV. Elizabeth slipped out the front door and into the night.

It was about two in the morning, but there was still a smattering of people here and there on the sidewalk. None of them were up to any good, the most harmless being the drunks, but they didn't concern Elizabeth. She moved furiously and briskly, feet beating on the sidewalk in rhythm, a woman with a mission, and people moved aside to avoid her. She was oblivious, being drawn toward something she could not define, but it was still familiar, oh so familiar. She'd experienced it too many times before. She had her hands jammed in her pockets, head down, bent slightly forward at the waist as she walked as if pushing a plow.

Her feet carried her through the streets, down sidewalks and around corners, through alleys, till she lost all track of where she was, but it didn't matter. When all this was done, she could always catch a cab or find a subway to get back to the hostel. For now, the silver thread connecting her to L. was singing to her and drawing tighter and tighter, pulling them together.

So that soon we may be one.

But that wasn't right. Elizabeth wasn't going to become one with L., she was going to capture her, and, if need be, kill her. It was just so hard...this part...the intimacy of sharing the mind was closer than that of a lover. At this stage, Elizabeth felt no revulsion toward her killers, only the need to be near them, to feel whole again. Once they were in sight of each other, identities could become defined again because Elizabeth would see them and know that they were not her and vice versa.

Her hands, balled into fists, still trembled a little. This was the hardest part, this was the shit that had landed her in the hospital more than once. The confusion, the sensations, not knowing if any of them were hers or even if she existed at all. Just the need to be whole and only by finding the one whose mind was inhabiting hers could she free herself, complete the circle.

She was over on the East side now in Alphabet City, and this was a dodgy neighborhood, but the way she walked and carried herself and perhaps the military clothing made the few people out and about continue to give her a wide berth. The wind had picked up, and her nose was growing cold. It smelled like snow though none was actually falling yet. One brick building, about four stories high, seemed to stand apart from the rest, a restless shifting thing that might change its form at any time if it fancied. Elizabeth had eyes only for that building, spotting it from three blocks away and it pulled her closer like a magnet till she was there then she stopped and looked up.

The top floor. Second window from the right.

The window she'd spotted was open like a mouth about to scream. The front door of the building was locked. That didn't stop her, couldn't stop her now. She waited a moment, wishing very hard, *needing* for the door to be unlocked and then tried it again. This time it opened. She stepped into the dark foyer, inner walls covered with looping, sprawling graffiti, no discernible pictures or words, just random chaotic markings. She made her way up the wooden stairs. The building was very quiet, and Elizabeth had no sense how many of these places were occupied and by what or by whom.

Rage was thrumming through her entire body now and her head hurt.

Is this what she feels like all the time?

Perhaps. Perhaps not.

At the top of the stairs, there were four apartments, two and two across from each other. The door of the one on the left with the open window was slightly ajar. At any other time, Elizabeth would have stopped, thinking that was strange, but she was no longer in complete control of herself. Something was compelling her forward.

She pushed the door open and entered. From the streetlight outside she could just make out the basic layout of the room. It appeared to be uninhabited and abandoned. There was a ripped old couch in the center of the room and an empty bookshelf against one wall but nothing else apart from a scattering of litter across the wooden floor. Still, the silence seemed alive somehow as if someone was there...hiding and watching. Waiting.

She drew her gun and held it close at her side, moving cautiously and slowly toward the back bedroom where the door was slightly open. Outside the door she pushed it open all the way. No sign of occupancy and the room was completely empty. She stepped inside to check the closets.

Wham! Something hit her hard on the back of the head. She staggered forward and fell, dropping her gun. Someone lunged forward, bent over and scooped up her gun. Instinctively, Elizabeth threw her hands over her head to protect herself from any further blows but whoever had hit her stepped back and away from her. When no more blows came, Elizabeth tentatively looked up. A small skinny figure stood pointing her own gun at her. Elizabeth recognized the elfin face and pointy features at once.

"L.," she said aloud.

The girl looked slightly confused but didn't respond to the use of the initial as a salutation.

"Who are you?" she asked instead, keeping the gun trained on Elizabeth. "And why have you been following me, appearing in my dreams?"

What? This had never happened before. None of Elizabeth's previous quarry had ever had any idea of her whereabouts or any clue as to how she'd located them. They'd certainly not been aware of her presence in their minds.

"What are you?" she asked, but that was a dumb question. Too late, she was beginning to get an inkling of what L. was—and why the Subset was interested.

"Shut up!" L. snapped. Her voice was trembling just faintly. "Answer my question."

"I'm Elizabeth Highsmith," Elizabeth answered truthfully, knowing that lying to L. was futile. "I'm a bounty hunter from Albuquerque. Where you killed that man."

L. spat on the floor. "Wasn't no man. He was a fucking animal, and he got exactly what he deserved."

Face-to-face with L., Elizabeth could now read her much more clearly, and she saw that L. *had* been telling the truth about the attack and the attempted rape. The kill in Albuquerque had been self-defense. But that still didn't explain…

"You kill others," she said.

L. shifted, the gun wavering a bit. She clearly hadn't expected Elizabeth to know this. "I kill those who deserve it," L. said finally. "It's still defense. Defense for women who can't or won't do it for themselves."

To Elizabeth's mind, this was all so much tired bullshit, a rationalization for something that was clearly personal and cathartic to L. and none of it answered what she wanted to know.

"How did you know I was coming?" she asked.

L. suddenly stepped forward and kicked her in the side as hard as she could. "I ask the questions, you dumb bitch! How did *you* know I was here?"

Elizabeth had rolled over and was clutching her side, fighting the urge to puke. It took her several moments to catch her breath so she could answer again.

"I just—I just knew."

It was the most unsatisfying answer she could have given, but it was the truth and L. seemed to understand that. "Yeah," she said, her voice soft again. "I just knew too."

Their eyes locked, Elizabeth still on the floor, and their faces wore identical expressions of confusion. What now? That was the question of the day.

Elizabeth understood L. to be a woman of action and oddly pragmatic. It didn't take her long to reach the logical conclusion. "I have to kill you," she said. Her voice sounded almost regretful. "I don't like killing women, but you shouldn't have followed me."

Elizabeth waited to feel something and couldn't. "I'd rather you didn't."

"Too bad."

L. had lowered the gun slightly. She raised it again now, pointing it at Elizabeth's head. Elizabeth closed her eyes. There was the sound of a gunshot, deafening and hurting Elizabeth's ears. L. screamed and there was a clattering sound as something fell to the ground. Elizabeth opened her eyes, startled. Her gun was lying in front of her. L. was hopping around, holding her hand, no longer screaming, her teeth clenched, face pale. Elizabeth saw blood gushing from the hand.

"What the hell?" Elizabeth uttered.

"Hello Mr. Elizabeth," a voice said. A woman wearing a black pantsuit stepped forward. Elizabeth recognized her from the NSA days. Captain Jane Leandra. She was holding a gun aimed at L. "You led us exactly where we hoped you would. Glad to see you haven't lost your touch. I heard you'd recovered but I didn't quite believe it. It's nice to be wrong."

Elizabeth pushed herself up so she was sitting on her knees and not feeling so vulnerable. "What are you doing here?" she asked.

"Looking for this one," Leandra said, nodding at L. "We knew she was out there but nothing else about her."

L. was looking wildly back and forth between them, trying to follow the conversation and unable to, but knowing that it didn't bode well, still holding her bleeding hand where Leandra had shot the gun away from her.

Two more figures in dark suits emerged from the shadows. They came and took L. by either arm. "Hello, Elizabeth," they said.

Elizabeth?

L. Short for Liz. Short for Elizabeth. The same as her. She sucked in her breath. This was too much.

"What do you want her for?" she asked.

"We don't waste talent," Leandra said. "And she's a natural. Same as you."

Elizabeth pushed herself to her feet, swaying slightly but wanting to be on equal footing with these people. "She's wanted for murder in Albuquerque."

"Not anymore," Leandra said. "Legally she is now dead. Tomorrow it will be official."

"What?" L.—Liz—squawked. "Who the fuck are you people?"

Leandra stepped forward and smacked L. across the face. "Your new employers. And the first thing you need to learn is that you don't speak unless spoken to."

"You'll be coming with us," one of the men holding an arm said softly. L. looked around desperately, catching Elizabeth's eye, and Elizabeth saw the panic and confusion and felt a strange moment of pity for L. But there was nothing to be done. This was bigger than both of them. It was Subset business, and she wanted no part of it.

"Fine," she said gruffly. "You got what you wanted out of me." She headed for the door. Right now, she wanted nothing more than a long hot shower, a good meal and a nap.

"Not so fast," Leandra said. "You're coming with us too."

"What?"

"Who do you think is going to train her?"

Elizabeth stared helplessly at Leandra then at L., the monster. Train this girl? She was a mess.

"You have to be kidding."

"We don't kid."

Elizabeth blinked, tears welling up. She was exhausted. Her mind had been stretched to the limit already and she needed sleep. And now her nightmare, the one she thought she'd escaped from two years ago, was proving to have never ended, was resuming all over again.

"I don't want to," she said, almost whispering.

"I know," Leandra said. "But you have no choice."

Elizabeth bowed her head and was quiet. There was nothing to be done. She was back with the Subset. And she'd be in close quarters with the human monster known as L.

"I hate you all," she murmured.

"We know."

There was nothing else to be said. Silently they left the building and went downstairs where a silver van was waiting outside. A burly man clad in black jumped out and opened the back doors of the van. They climbed in the van and it drove away into the night.

CHAPTER FOUR

From a bird's-eye view, the landscape is untouched. Rolling green hills with a scattering of trees in between. Only by zooming in closer does the rape of the land become apparent, and it is a subtle thing, the damage carefully concealed to all but the most discerning eye. The complex is large and sprawling but almost entirely underground. There will be no unwanted light entering these premises. Sliding metal doors appear incongruously in the various jutting hilltops. If you were granted access to these sliding metal doors, they would take you deep underground where the real action occurs. They would take you to the Basement. You do not want access to these sliding doors. If you encountered them, if you were wise, you would let your feet carry you away from them, running not walking.

Unfortunately, Liz and Elizabeth had no choice but to be here.

The entire complex encompassed over a square mile of land and the Basement was comprised of many rooms, all of them used for different purposes. Some of them harbored strange and beautiful and dangerous things; others were empty, waiting for their purpose to be fulfilled. Liz and Elizabeth were in one of these rooms.

The room was a refurbished gym. The floor was hardwood and the markings of a basketball court were still upon it and nets hung from backboards on either side. Had the room ever been used for something as innocent as a gym or was this just one more psychological trick of the Subset, designed for some obscure purpose? One could never be sure and it didn't pay to think about it too much. Wooden bleachers were folded back, pressed almost fearfully against either wall. There was a toilet located against the far wall under one of the basketball nets. A large supply of toilet paper rested nearby. There was no covering for the toilet, no privacy for whoever needed to use it. Just one more detail of how the Subset fully intended to break down all barriers, take away even the most basic options of privacy. *We own you and do not forget it.* Two cots had been set up on opposite sides of the gym, lengthwise. At the foot of each cot was a military locker and if the lockers had been opened, each would have revealed seven identical pairs of gray sweatsuits, seven pairs of sports bras and white cotton underwear, and seven pairs of white socks. A large metal box the approximate size and shape of a vending machine rested against the wall on the opposite side of the gym, the same wall as the toilet. Several large speakers were mounted up in the corners of the ceiling. Rows of fluorescent lights glared down mercilessly.

On one cot, Elizabeth lay unconscious, dressed in a gray sweatsuit. Liz was unconscious on the other cot, dressed the same.

Unseen, but always there, up in the far corners of the ceiling near the speakers, were small cameras, no larger than the nail of a pinky finger, the latest technology, recording everything. Watching. And waiting. For soon the show would begin, and the Subset wanted to miss nothing. Elizabeth was not their first choice for a trainer, but she was the only one who had been able to pick up Liz's frequency. Ergo, she was the only one who could train her. They were not unaware of Liz's extracurricular activities but that was incidental, of no great concern to them. They had men and women on the payroll who had done far worse, and such minor character defects they believed could always be reshaped, and ultimately utilized for the greater good. And if she could not be retrained, that would be a shame, for a great deal of money and hope was going into this, but in the end, Liz, like Elizabeth, indeed like all of them, was expendable. For the greater good must always come first.

Now though, all was silent, and the two figures slept on. The camera recorded everything.

* * *

The spiders came first. Elizabeth felt them crawling over her, but she didn't know what they were. Her head felt heavy and strange, her tongue thick and furry. Her last memory was outside the abandoned apartment. Liz had been there and then the Subset. They'd told her she needed to train Liz, hadn't they, and then they'd hustled both of them out to the back of the van. In the van, they'd been met by two large men wearing all white and then there had been sharpness, a needle sliding into the side of her neck with a quick painful stick, and everything had grown dark.

She managed to raise an arm that felt as if it were made of taffy and brushed at her cheek. Something light with small feet scampered away down the side of her face. She opened her eyes. Spiders. Everywhere. Tarantulas. They were crawling over her, crawling over the floor of the gym. Hundreds of them, no, thousands of them, and they all had red eyes.

"Aggghh!"

She jumped up, swaying a little, nearly blacking out but her panic sent a burst of adrenaline to her brain, and she stayed standing, brushing the spiders off her. One started to climb up her sneaker (*Sneaker? Where did sneakers come from? Wasn't I wearing boots?*) Elizabeth raised her foot and frantically shook it off then stomped on it. Guts splattered everywhere, and she felt the slight resistance and squishiness under her shoe. That quickly dispelled any notion she might have had about this being a dream. She looked around wildly, having no idea where she was, but taking it all in quick enough. Her eyes landed on Liz, still asleep on her cot. There were no spiders on Liz. In fact, the spiders gave her area wide berth, about five feet of empty space on every side. Without thinking, Elizabeth ran over, stepping on the tarantulas as she went, not caring, just wanting to get away from them. She reached Liz's cot, grabbed the woman's shoulder and shook it.

"Wake up!" she screamed.

Liz whimpered once, arms flying up even before her eyes opened, then sat bolt upright, fists clenched, ready to fight, looking around wildly. Her eyes landed on Elizabeth, and they were full of hatred.

"You!"

Elizabeth opened her mouth. She had no idea what she was about to say. Help me? We have to get out of here? It didn't matter. The spiders had vanished. The moment Liz had woken up, they'd flickered out of existence as if they'd never been. Except they had been. They'd been real, all right. Elizabeth felt herself trembling. She backed away from Liz, blinking quickly. She would not cry. This was not the time. She had dealt once with the Subset, and she could deal with them again.

Pull yourself together, roared a deep masculine voice in her head. Elizabeth dug her fingernails into her arm and yanked down, tearing off skin, but the pain grounded her. Her tears receded. She took a deep breath and one last wary glance at the ground, then her legs folded under her and she sat on the floor.

"You were dreaming," she said tiredly.

Liz just sat there for a couple of moments, staring straight ahead, looking as shellshocked as Elizabeth felt, then swung her legs over the side of the cot and looked at Elizabeth. Her expression was partly defiant but underneath, Elizabeth could see the fear and the uncertainty.

"Where are we?" she asked.

This, at least, Elizabeth could answer. "You're in custody of the Subset," she said. "They're a branch of the government, a subset of the National Security Agency. They recruit from all military branches and even the private sector, but I don't think they're really *of* the military though they work closely together."

Liz scowled. "What do they want with *me?*" she asked. "I'm nobody."

Elizabeth crossed her legs and rested her head in her hands. It suddenly seemed too heavy to hold up. She wanted to go back to sleep. "They think you might possess certain psychic abilities."

"*What?*" Liz let out one short bark of laughter. "Gimme a fuckin' break! If I was psychic, don't you think I'd be rich? I'd be living at the casino, raking in the dough. Trust me, I'm not psychic."

Elizabeth felt a surge of rage, mostly because she used to think the same sort of thing.

"All that shit you see in the movies?" she said. "About psychics reading minds and carrying on conversations without talking? Well, it's bullshit. Fucking bullshit! It doesn't work that way. If it did, I'd be rich too. It's something you have no control over, and it manifests in all kinds of different ways."

Liz still looked wary but intrigued too. "Like how?"

"Like how I found you. I didn't know your name or where you lived. I don't know when I'm reading your mind because a thought is a thought so I'm never sure if it's your thought or mine that I'm picking up. Occasionally there's a random image, but for the most part, it's all simply very strong intuition. I just *knew* where to find you. As simple as that. We share a frequency."

"I could feel someone in my mind a few months ago," Liz said slowly. "But at the same time…I just thought I was being paranoid. I can…get that way."

"Yeah, well, this time you weren't," Elizabeth said, watching Liz carefully. She was impressed by the girl's acceptance of the situation. Liz was shaken but she seemed to be handling it all well.

Seemed to be. A moment later, Liz ruined that impression. She jumped up and ran to the two metal doors at the end of the gymnasium. They were padlocked shut and made of solid metal but that didn't stop her from yanking on them and shaking them. And this, despite the small bandage on her hand. The gunshot had not penetrated her hand, just grazed the flesh leaving a relatively minor wound that someone had bandaged while she was unconscious.

"Lemme outta here!" she screamed. "Lemme the fuck out of here! I'll sue, I swear to God!"

Elizabeth closed her eyes, feeling her headache getting worse. She didn't bother to go after Liz. Eventually she would realize the futility of what she was doing, but she might as well let her burn herself out this way and get it out of her system.

The girl had no quit in her. She kept it up for a good solid two hours and even after her voice grew hoarse, she still kept it up. No common sense apparently but you had to give her points for heart. Elizabeth, lying on her cot, wondered when and how they'd be fed and tried to tune out Liz's hollering. She also wondered how she was supposed to train this girl. Presumably it was to teach her to get control of her gift, but that was a joke considering Elizabeth had only minimal control of her own abilities. Although she supposed that was better than none. Or maybe…maybe just the close proximity of her to Liz was enough to trigger and strengthen both their talents and perhaps that was what the Subset wanted. Whoever knew with them? They'd let her know when and if they were good and ready.

Finally, Liz left the doors and strode over to Elizabeth. She still looked angry and her fists were clenched. She stood, hands on hips, looking down at Elizabeth on the cot.

"You're awfully accepting of this," she said, her voice accusatory.

Elizabeth shrugged. "What can we do?" she said wearily.

Useless, Liz thought. Elizabeth reminded her of a dead slug. She was the last person she would have chosen to be stuck with. Well, Elizabeth could passively accept this all she wanted; Liz had no intention of staying here. She looked around the room carefully. There wasn't much to see. It looked like a standard gymnasium with two cots and the incongruity of a toilet under a basketball net. She looked up at the ceiling. A couple of vents, but too high and centered to reach even if they hauled out the bleachers and stood on them. No windows at all. She looked at Elizabeth's cot and noticed for the first time that it was bolted to the floor. There would be no moving the cots or taking them apart to use the legs as weapons, assuming that someone came to feed them or speak to them or do anything else with them.

She walked over to the metal box that resembled a vending machine and inspected it. There was a slot where food would be dispensed if it were a vending machine but there was no area in which to put money. Liz knelt down on the wooden floor and tried to peer under the machine. It went all the way to the floor. She stood up and pushed against it as hard as she could. It didn't move.

"Come help me!" she called to Elizabeth.

Elizabeth didn't move. "Why?" she called back, sounding tired.

Liz scowled and turned back to the machine, not bothering to answer. If Elizabeth couldn't understand the importance of doing something then she was worse than useless. She herself always did things; you had to fight back, even if you were doomed to lose, *especially* if you were doomed to lose. Fighting back was sometimes all you had. It was usually, at least in her case, all she had. She kicked at the machine as hard as she could. The lights flickered once then went off. The gym was swallowed by darkness. Liz stared ahead, unable to even see the machine that she knew was less than a foot in front of her face. She put out one hand tentatively and felt the cold metal of the machine beneath her fingertips. She kicked it again.

A high whistling sound began emanating from the speakers. It sounded like nails on a chalkboard. Liz winced and covered her ears.

"Would you stop it?" Elizabeth screamed furiously.

"I'm not doing it!" Liz yelled back.

"If you hadn't been kicking that damn thing!" Elizabeth hollered.

The unfairness of this infuriated Liz. At least she'd been *trying* to do something not just lying passively on her cot like a slug.

"At least I try!" she yelled, running in the direction of Elizabeth's voice. She didn't know what she'd do when she got there, but she was so enraged she didn't care. She was sure she'd think of something.

It was hard running in the dark but something instinctively told her where she was, and she was more sure-footed than most people. It was the high-pitched screeching sound that was aggravating her, making her want to rip and tear and bite and punch until it just shut the hell up.

Even with the screeching, Elizabeth could hear the thumping of Liz's sneakers on the wooden floor as she ran. Elizabeth sat up, fists clenched, enraged. Stupid girl! If it weren't for her, Elizabeth would still be at home in New Mexico, safe in her house with her books and her computer games. The sneakers pounded closer and closer and then something—Liz—leapt on her. Elizabeth was ready and grabbed her. They rolled on the floor, throwing wild punches in the dark. The screeching sound suddenly stopped. Elizabeth felt Liz's hands let go of her and, feeling suddenly foolish, she let go of Liz.

"What the hell?" Liz said.

They were still in the dark so Elizabeth could hear Liz, even her breathing, next to her, but couldn't see her. "Just another game of the Subset," Elizabeth said sourly.

"I still don't understand what they want with me," Liz said.

Elizabeth didn't say anything. She was beginning to wonder that herself. Initially she'd thought "assassin" because of her dream but when she thought more about it, that didn't really make sense. If they wanted someone assassinated, all they had to do was give an order; there was no need for so complex a situation as this. No, whatever the reason they wanted Liz, it was bigger than a simple assassination. But what was bigger than assassination? Elizabeth didn't know; she'd stopped using her imagination after she'd left the military. The events she'd seen had surpassed anything her imagination could ever have come up with, and she'd discovered there was such a thin boundary between perception and reality that she no longer enjoyed playing with such concepts. As a result, she conceded her imagination could only be described as rusty.

"Train her," a voice boomed out over the loudspeaker, making both women jump.

Nerves still on edge and frayed, Elizabeth instinctively did the only thing she could think of to do: she lashed out at Liz in her mind, picturing her fist knocking the girl in the air and to the floor.

She wasn't prepared for the backlash. A force suddenly grabbed her and threw her back through the dark several feet into the air. She flailed, trying to balance herself and came down hard on her wrist, bending it back. She heard the loud crack and at first felt nothing, then suddenly the world was full of pain and her wrist was on fire.

"Ahhh..." She made a tiny whimper and sucked in air.

"What the hell was that?" Liz asked.

"My wrist," Elizabeth said tightly. "You broke it."

"How?"

"I don't know."

She heard Liz approaching her and then suddenly the lights in the gym flooded back on, and there was Liz standing over her, then squatting down, looking concerned and confused.

"What did you *do*?" Liz asked, putting emphasis on the last word.

Elizabeth shook her head. "When that voice said to train you...I just got so sick of the whole thing and you that I tried —mentally—to smack you. Then something hit me and I was flying through the air."

"That's what that was," Liz said, sounding delighted and pleased with herself for having figured something out. "I felt something coming at me so I just pictured this massive bullet-proof glass wall being erected and zooming forth to meet it."

"Well, it worked," Elizabeth said ruefully.

Liz smiled. "Is this what training is going to be like?" she asked.

"Let's hope not," Elizabeth said. Her face had grown very pale, the circles under the eyes more pronounced. She was in agony from her wrist. Liz finally remembered and her face crinkled in concern as she looked at Elizabeth.

"Your wrist!" she cried, and instinctively looked around for something to use as a splint. There was nothing. The wrist was bent at an unnatural angle. She was sure it felt much worse than it looked.

Elizabeth, meanwhile, had managed to push the pain to one side. It wasn't as if she was no longer feeling it, but it was all off to one side now, and she could concentrate on other things. In fact, it helped if she concentrated on other things. She studied Liz's face and tried to remember that this young-looking girl killed people. It was getting harder and harder to remember. She should be afraid of Liz, even if she could only feel that fear on an intellectual level, and yet she wasn't.

Liz was studying the wrist, her tongue poking out slightly in concentration. "I can fix that," she said finally and her voice was cheerful again.

Elizabeth was beginning to get enough sense of Liz to realize that she was delighting not in the fact that the wrist was broken but that there was something she could do about it.

Liz's hands suddenly darted out, seized Elizabeth's hand and wrist—how hot her hands were!—and then yanked. Elizabeth screamed. This time the pain could not be ignored. It lasted only a few seconds, but those seconds seemed to drag on interminably. Elizabeth's eyes filled with tears. She realized she still knew how to cry. When she was younger, how easy tears had come, embarrassingly so, along with blushing. It seemed to her she had spent the majority of her teens either sopping wet with tears or beet red with embarrassment or both. She'd been relieved to outgrow *that* though it had seemed to take forever. She blinked back the tears now, not letting them fall and hoped she wouldn't black out. Her head felt very light, the skin on her body too tight. She lowered her head between her knees.

"Are you all right?" Liz asked.

"Give me a minute. I'll be fine."

Sure enough, after a few minutes, her head began to clear and she felt better. The wrist still hurt but it was no longer as painful. Elizabeth concentrated on healing it, sending instructions to her cells to reknit the bones. She couldn't do it all at once but she could speed up the process. Years ago when she'd been assaulted in New York, one of the few times she'd been unable to avoid danger, she'd had two of her ribs broken. She'd managed to limp to the bathroom, clean herself up and tape the ribs—which was almost more painful than having them broken—and then healed them in two weeks. This would all be easier if she had something to hold the wrist in place but if she had to, she could make do without.

"You look a little better. Less pale," Liz commented finally.

Elizabeth nodded. "I'm feeling better. Somewhat."

A broken wrist was still a broken wrist and even with her high tolerance for pain, at least of the physical variety and her ability to compartmentalize, the wrist hurt but it was manageable for now if she could just keep it still. She realized she'd be very helpless for a while and thus dependent upon Liz. The thought made her uncomfortable, and she studied Liz carefully, taking in the expressive, large, dark eyes, the unruly shaggy brown hair, narrow face and the light smattering of freckles across her face. Liz had a surprisingly innocent, friendly-looking face considering all the criminality she'd done and all that had been done to her. Elizabeth did not like her still, but she was beginning to find her less repulsive and somewhat…intriguing. Was it possible, she wondered, to reform a murderer? Was Liz really a sociopath or just horribly damaged? Was there a difference? Maybe the answer to whether sociopaths were born or made was not a cut-and-dried definitive answer but varied from person to person. No doubt some were born that way. Maybe others were made that way: people who could have gone either way at birth, impressionable people who adapted all too fully to their environments and gave back exactly what they got, be that good or bad.

Liz shifted a little under Elizabeth's scrutiny, looking self-conscious. "Whatcha' lookin' at?"

"You," Elizabeth admitted.

"How come?"

"Just trying to figure you out."

Liz laughed. "Good luck. I've been working on that one for

years and still no luck. If you succeed, will you let me know?"

Elizabeth found herself unexpectedly responding to Liz's smile and smiling back. "Absolutely."

There was a whirring sound from the machine. Both women jumped and looked toward it. Part of the metal in the front casing slid back revealing a small door. Inside were two food trays side by side.

"Food!" Liz yelled happily and ran toward it.

Elizabeth followed, moving more gingerly because of her wrist. Liz handed Elizabeth her tray before taking her own. The trays were plastic, the kind found in school cafeterias the world over, and the food itself did not look much more appetizing. Two thin slices of turkey on each tray with brown gravy on them, a scoop of instant mashed potatoes in another compartment, watery green beans, and a small square of what looked vaguely like cherry pie, which Elizabeth had never cared for, believing fruits and desserts should never be mixed. There was also a wrapped plastic knife, fork, spoon and napkin alongside each tray and two pints of milk in waxy cardboard.

"Yum," Elizabeth said flatly, taking her tray with her good arm.

Liz looked more enthusiastic as she eyed her tray. "I ain't complaining. This is better than I've eaten in months. Real meat!"

Elizabeth, who'd been a vegetarian for the last seven years, didn't answer. She was hungry enough that she wondered how long her vegetarianism would last. Principles were all well and good but when it came to starving or eating meat, she had a feeling she'd revert back to being a carnivore soon enough.

She carried her tray to her cot and sat down, balancing the tray on her lap. To her surprise, rather than returning to her own cot, Liz followed and sat down on the floor near Elizabeth's feet, cross-legged, her tray in front of her. Elizabeth picked up her utensils then realized she had no way of opening the plastic bag in which they were contained. She held it for a moment, just looking at it, frustrated by her own helplessness.

Liz saw her dilemma and hopped up. "Let me help you," she said.

Elizabeth felt strange to be accepting help from Liz, vulnerable and naked in a way, but as she had no choice, she just nodded. Liz tore open the utensils and handed Elizabeth the fork, setting the others back on the tray. "Do you want me to cut up your meat?" she asked.

"I don't eat meat. I'm a vegetarian," she said.

Liz stared at her as if she'd announced something bizarre. "Why?" she asked.

Elizabeth shrugged, feeling more self-conscious than ever. "I love animals. I don't like the way they're treated when they're raised for food. It's one thing to hunt them in the wild, but the way they're bred and treated in captivity is beyond inhumane."

Liz looked intrigued then abruptly smiled as if she'd discovered something amusing. "You're an old softy!" she crowed in delight. "Who would have guessed? You come across like a crusty old bitch, but underneath it, you're a big marshmallow."

Elizabeth, who hadn't been aware that she came across like a "crusty old bitch" had to laugh as well, as much at Liz's guilelessness as at her words.

"Can I have your turkey?" Liz asked.

Elizabeth nodded, and Liz transferred the turkey to her own tray with her knife and fork. She opened Elizabeth's milk for her and then both of them settled down to eat for the first time in at least twenty-four hours, and there was no more talking for a while. Liz finished first, despite having more food. She ate like a starving animal, barely chewing her food before gulping it down. After she was done, she belched with contentment. "Compliments to the chef," she said. "Now if I only had a smoke, life would be good."

Inwardly, Elizabeth had to marvel at Liz's ability to adapt. In less than two days, she'd been ambushed, kidnapped, had her life completely taken away from her, and yet here she was, content with a few pieces of mediocre turkey, and her only complaint was the lack of cigarettes.

Elizabeth wondered what would happen next, but the question was answered for her when the overhead lights were flicked off, and they were plunged back into darkness. "I hope that means bedtime and not more trouble," she remarked dryly. Liz laughed but it sounded decidedly lackluster.

"Can you find your way back to your cot?" Elizabeth asked, concerned, remembering that Liz was all the way across the gym. She thought it was strange that the cots should be so far apart rather than close together, but then this whole situation was strange.

"Yeah," Liz answered.

Elizabeth waited but there was no sound of movement from Liz. "Good night," she said finally.

Liz got the message. "Good night," she answered, and Elizabeth heard her getting up and moving across the gym, then more sounds of her lying down on her cot.

She shifted on her own, careful not to move her broken wrist, and managed to find a moderately comfortable position. She expected to be awake for a long time but to her surprise, perhaps because it had been such an exhausting day, she found herself falling asleep quickly.

Some indeterminate time later, she woke to the sound of screams in the darkness. They were screams of pure terror. Elizabeth jerked awake, feeling hands all over her. She flailed her arms to beat them off, forgetting about her wrist then screamed in agony as pain shot through her whole arm. The hands disappeared but Elizabeth could still hear Liz screaming over on her cot.

"Liz!" she yelled. "Are you all right?"

The screams subsided. There was silence for perhaps a minute.

"Elizabeth?" Liz finally replied. Her voice sounded very small in the darkness.

"What's wrong?"

"I dunno."

Elizabeth waited, but Liz had nothing else to add. Something in the air left Elizabeth feeling that Liz was unusually subdued, but she didn't know her well enough to really press the issue. She lay back down on her cot instead, her body still tense. Then she sat up in the dark, picturing Liz curled on her side on the cot across the gym and wondered what had set her off. Liz had too many issues for her to make any guess.

"Elizabeth?" Liz's voice came right next to Elizabeth's cot and sounded uncertain.

"Yes?"

"Can I sleep on the floor next to you? I don't—I don't like the dark."

Elizabeth thought of her gun at home on her bedside table and how she slept with it every night. Maybe she didn't like the dark either.

"Sure."

She heard Liz bustling around in the dark next to her, felt the draft from a blanket as it was fanned out and laid down, then the pillows being tossed on the floor. She reached down with her good arm to see where Liz had ended up and felt a very warm hand take hold of her own. The contact was strange but not unpleasant. Again, Elizabeth felt that strangely naked vulnerable feeling that Liz too easily seemed able to give her.

She's half your age, she reminded herself, not knowing why she did so, but even that wasn't true. If Liz was in her early to mid-twenties then she was between ten and fifteen years younger than Elizabeth at most. They were closer in age to being sisters than parent and child, though right now Liz seemed very child-like.

"Good night," Liz murmured, her voice sounding more relaxed, younger, and very sleepy.

"Good night," Elizabeth answered, not sure if it would be impolite to extricate her hand and not sure if she even wanted to. It made it more difficult for her to get back to sleep, her hand dangling off the cot, held by Liz, but eventually she managed and then both women slept silently for the rest of the night, hand in hand.

CHAPTER FIVE

The next morning, or what she assumed was morning, Elizabeth woke up when Liz removed her hand and quickly stood up. Liz looked around the room which was lighted again, looked at everything everywhere except for Elizabeth's eyes. Which just annoyed Elizabeth. Last night she'd felt almost protective of Liz, fond of her.

"I want a fuckin' cigarette," Liz said and her voice was loud. She was back to her old brash self, brasher and louder than before.

Elizabeth sat up, irritated though she didn't know why. She'd *known* Liz had issues. Why should she be surprised that Liz would slip back to her old ways after opening herself and being vulnerable? Nonetheless it *did* irritate her because she'd begun to feel close to Liz, as if she were beginning to get to know her, maybe even to become friends, and now the door was shut again, all defenses up. One step forward and two steps back, that was apparently Liz and it made Elizabeth want to shake the girl.

"Well, we don't have them," Elizabeth snapped, and Liz glowered at her. Elizabeth recoiled at the pure rage and hatred in Liz's eyes.

What the hell did I do?

You were nice to her.

Yes, but why—

Liz kicked at her cot and though it was bolted to the floor, the motion startled Elizabeth enough that she fell off the cot backward. She hit her head and her wrist slammed against the wooden gym floor. She screamed with the pain.

"Elizabeth!" Suddenly Liz was above her, all dark eyes and stricken face, looking about to cry. "I'm so—"

The door to the gym burst open. Six men in full black protective gear, including helmets with visors burst in, carrying rifles. Elizabeth felt dizzy with pain, but she watched through the haze of wavering lines as the six men thundered toward them on booted feet, seized Liz and then one stepped forward, swinging his rifle and catching Liz in the stomach. Liz doubled over and dropped to her knees, then hunched forward. Another man (or maybe it was a woman under there, who could be sure?) stepped forward, kicking her.

"Stop it!" Elizabeth screamed. It was one thing to see such things in her mind, even to know that Liz had surely taken such beatings before just as Elizabeth had, but it was another to watch it being done to her, the pure savagery of it making Elizabeth sick. She turned away, dry heaving, as they kept at Liz, pounding her. Liz never made a sound. That didn't impress Elizabeth. It just told her how out of touch Liz was with her own body, though no doubt it felt like some kind of victory to not give them the satisfaction of exhibiting pain. How much practice must that have taken? To Elizabeth, Liz just looked little and helpless, being beaten. No matter what she'd done, she didn't deserve this. She was a disturbed girl/woman who'd snapped at Elizabeth and kicked a cot when she felt angry and uncertain about her feelings; hardly behavior worthy of this savagery.

After a few minutes that seemed to go on forever, one of the figures leaned down and spoke in a low voice into Liz's ear but Elizabeth was close enough that she could hear.

"From now on, you keep your hands and feet to yourself when you're angry. Got it?"

Liz, hunched over in a ball, didn't answer. The figure straightened and kicked her hard in the thigh. "Got it?" he snapped again.

"Yes," Liz answered in a low voice.

"Good."

He fell in with the others and they all marched out of the gym in formation, the door slamming shut and locking behind them.

Her earlier anger and even the pain in her wrist had vanished. Elizabeth managed to stumble to her feet using her one good arm and made her way over to Liz who was still hunched over on the gym floor. She knelt down and placed her hand gently on the nape of Liz's neck.

"Is anything broken? Are you all right?" she asked and her voice was gentler than ever before with Liz.

Perhaps that accounted for Liz's reaction. She didn't answer, but reached over, putting her arms around Elizabeth's waist and burying her face against her thighs. Elizabeth could feel her trembling. It seemed Liz was not nearly so tough as she tried to appear. Elizabeth softly stroked her hair and her back. For the first time, it occurred to her that they were in this together. Both of them were victims and it didn't matter whose "fault" it was that they were here. They needed each other to survive.

Maybe this is what they wanted of you?

No doubt it was, and Elizabeth was being manipulated perfectly but just because the situation had been engineered to achieve a desired effect did not make it any less true or real.

She sat there silently, stroking Liz's hair for a while, reflecting on the situation and gradually feeling her strength come back to her. Not her physical strength but her mental strength which had been flagging ever since this adventure began. Now she realized that much of what had felt like being overwhelmed had been simple whining and self-pity. It did not matter if she "wanted" to deal with the Subset again or not. The situation was what it was, and she could either deal with it or sit and feel sorry for herself, but nothing was going to change unless she made it change.

There was also Liz. Initially she had dismissed Liz as a human monster, beyond redemption, and not worthy of any further thought. Now, for the first time, she could see her as a human being, however disturbed, and far more vulnerable than the young woman wanted to believe of herself or admit. Elizabeth did not have a maternal bone in her body—or at least she liked to claim so—and no interest in children, but Liz, at this moment, did provoke some protective feeling in her that at the very least, if not maternal, could certainly be described as sisterly. She felt compassion for her. Sympathy. She did not see a monster or creature anymore, just an injured person in pain who needed help and a lot of it.

Oh honey. I'm a mess too. But still…in the house of the blind, maybe the one-eyed man is indeed king.

She stroked Liz's hair, a rather bemused smile on her face, and Liz stirred a little.

"Thank you," she murmured, sitting up.

Elizabeth winced, finally catching sight of Liz's face. Her lower lip was swollen and cracked and her left eye was also swollen shut, the outer edge bright red which would no doubt be a nasty purple bruise within a few hours.

"You look like hell," she said tenderly.

Liz shrugged and stood up. "I've taken worse," she said coolly, and Elizabeth felt a surge of exasperation and affection for this girl who was so determined to be macho and tough.

"Anytime you wanna drop the macho bullshit act, you can," she said mildly. The words were harsh but the tone was so inoffensive that Liz just looked surprised rather than angry.

"What do you mean?"

"This…act you do," Elizabeth said, waving her good hand, trying to explain. "I'll admit…part of me admires it, but another part of me just finds it sad. I get it. You're tough. We all know that. But it's okay not to be indifferent to your own pain."

Liz winced. Somehow Elizabeth's words had reached her. And despite her own laconic nature, so similar to Elizabeth, she managed to get her own point of view across when she replied.

"I have to survive," she said, just as mildly, and that statement, with all that it encompassed, hit home for Elizabeth, and she understood. Liz did what she could, and if bullshit machismo had kept her going and alive throughout her short and painful life then maybe it wasn't bullshit. At the very least, Elizabeth could not belittle it.

"Fair enough," she said.

Liz suddenly came over and knelt directly beside Elizabeth, and very gently took hold of her broken wrist. The touch did not hurt. Those startlingly warm hands were surprisingly tender, but Elizabeth gasped anyway, feeling a quick wave of residual fear.

"What are you doing?"

"Close your eyes," Liz said firmly.

Elizabeth gave her one wary look and then, despite her misgivings, closed her eyes. The wrist was still throbbing, a dull faraway ache. As she sat there, she felt the wrist heating up under Liz's hands and could picture a yellow glow slowly unfurling around it, warming it, starting to swirl, gently at first then more frantically. This went on for what she guessed was ten minutes. Then suddenly Liz's hands disappeared and the warmth went away too.

"Open your eyes," Liz ordered.

Elizabeth obeyed. Her wrist no longer hurt. Gingerly she held it up and looked at it. Then she bent it and moved it with no difficulty at all. Her mouth fell open.

"You healed it!"

Liz smiled, looking very pleased with herself. Elizabeth smiled back, still feeling shocked. "How did you do that?"

"I don't know," Liz admitted. "I just suddenly felt like if I concentrated I could heal it."

Elizabeth was quiet because she was remembering the cat. Because she knew what Liz was talking about. In her apartment complex years ago, back in New York, there had been a cat that had fallen from a fifth-story window onto the sidewalk below. Everyone who saw it had run outside, but Elizabeth had reached it first. The cat had been lying on its side, not breathing, legs straight out and stiff. Elizabeth had placed her hands on its side and *willed* it to breathe, and a moment later the cat had been gasping, breathing rapidly and quickly but still breathing. Elizabeth told herself the cat had been in shock, its breath knocked out of it and that her touch had simply stimulated it, but deep down, hadn't she known better, even then? That cat had been just as dead as a turd when she found it; she'd brought it back. It was like the butterfly she'd found on the sidewalk in high school. Elizabeth had picked it up by one wing, marveling at is beauty and then for some reason she could not explain, she'd breathed on it and the butterfly had fluttered away, just as pretty as you please. Elizabeth had never told anyone about either of these incidents. Not the true version anyway; some things you simply *can't* share.

"Thank you," Elizabeth said, standing up. She should have felt happy and pleased, and certainly she *was* happy that her wrist no longer hurt, and she wouldn't be dependent on Liz for everything, but something about the whole incident also made her uncomfortable. It bothered her that Liz could simultaneously be a killer and a healer. It meant the neat boundaries Elizabeth had drawn in her head that divided human from monster, good from bad, were perhaps not so clearly delineated as she'd made them.

"I'm going to use the toilet," she said. "Don't peek."

Liz just rolled her eyes. Feeling a little stupid and very self-conscious, Elizabeth went and used the toilet under the basketball net. Liz discreetly kept her back turned, but at one point, Elizabeth was sure she saw her peeking and smirking. Afterward, Liz also went and used the toilet. Elizabeth waited by her cot, and then, just for payback, turned and looked. Liz, sitting on the throne, simply smiled and waved. "Liking the show, are you, luv?" she hollered in a bad Cockney accent. Elizabeth turned away again but couldn't help laughing. It was hard to keep Liz down. Her macho act perhaps wasn't such an act; she really *was* that tough.

After their morning pee, Elizabeth lay back on her cot for a quick nap while Liz jogged laps around the gym to help get rid of her craving for a cigarette. The soft thud of her feet on the wood floor of the gym was rhythmic and surprisingly soothing. Elizabeth quickly fell asleep and slept longer than she'd intended. It wasn't until lunch, when she heard the whirring of the machine, that she woke up. Lunch was a cheeseburger, chips, milk and more green beans. Liz plowed in with her usual gusto, and Elizabeth slipped her the burger, reflecting as she did that she might be losing a few extra pounds here, and Liz would perhaps gain a few much needed ones.

"That was delicious," Liz said, her mouth still full as she finished her last bite.

"Don't talk with your mouth full," Elizabeth corrected absentmindedly. In response, Liz opened her mouth wide like a twelve-year-old, showing off all her chewed-up food. Elizabeth rolled her eyes and laughed. "You're hopeless."

Liz laughed back, happy to have made Elizabeth laugh. "That's what they say."

After lunch, Elizabeth was bored again. "I wish we had cards or something," she said. It was an obvious complaint and Liz, looking cranky, probably from nicotine withdrawal, didn't bother to answer. Elizabeth went to lie back down on her cot. Liz started jogging. The lights overhead flickered on and off once.

"Train her," the voice boomed from the loudspeaker, somehow managing to sound like a very loud whisper.

Liz and Elizabeth looked at each other warily. The lights flickering were clearly a warning, and neither wanted to ignore it. Liz touched her swollen eye and glanced nervously toward the door.

"We'd better do what they say," she said.

You learn quick, Elizabeth thought, but there was no need to say that aloud especially as part of her admired the spunk Liz had shown in resisting the Subset. Futile or not, the girl had determination and heart. She sat up. "All right. Let's do this."

"What should we start with?" Liz asked.

"I don't know," Elizabeth admitted. "The problem is I don't know exactly what you can do. I don't even know all that I can do. Why don't we try blocks like we did yesterday?"

"Blocks?"

"Where I tried to hit you mentally and you blocked me. But go easy," she added quickly, not in any hurry to have her wrist broken again.

Liz nodded, looking dubious. "I'll try," she said.

"Okay. You go over to your cot and stand in front of it, and I'll stand in front of mine," Elizabeth said. "You try and hit me, and then I'll try and hit you and so forth."

Liz nodded and trotted across the gym to her abandoned cot—she'd taken up permanent residence it seemed on the floor by Elizabeth's cot—and then stood in front of it.

"Okay. One...two...three...go!" Elizabeth yelled.

She felt what could only be described as a rush of air heading toward her though nothing moved and mentally threw up a metal wall to block it. She felt it bounce off and head back to Liz. What Liz did, she didn't know, but suddenly the walls shook and the ceiling cracked. Both women looked up in shock. The lights abruptly flicked off.

"Elizabeth?" Liz yelled.

"I'm over here!"

She heard Liz running across the gym and then felt her arm grabbed as Liz moved next to her. Liz's hands were trembling.

She *really* doesn't like the dark, Elizabeth thought, and instinctively put an arm around Liz who was shaking. Liz sank gratefully against Elizabeth, and in the dark, with only touch and weight to guide her, Elizabeth was abruptly aware of how physically tiny Liz actually was. She herself was only five foot-three, one hundred and forty pounds, but she felt mammoth in comparison, and felt strangely protective of Liz. In the daylight, Liz's loud mouth and swaggering attitude made her seem bigger than she actually was, but in the dark, her physical limitations were painfully apparent. She had been fighting a losing battle from the start. The idea of six people beating on a five-foot, one-hundred-pound girl made her even sicker now than it had at the time, and that had felt bad enough.

The words that came out of her mouth next were spoken in a whisper and surprised even her. "We have to get out of here."

If Liz was surprised, considering Elizabeth's previous acceptance of the situation, she didn't show it. She adapted quickly.

"How?" she murmured back.

"Concentrate on the far wall," Elizabeth said. She sensed Liz nodding next to her, and her arm still around the girl, she whispered: "One...two...three!"

They both concentrated on the far wall. Elizabeth had never done anything like this before, but she'd never been in the presence of someone like Liz before either. Together, their powers seemed double what they were when each was alone. Was that why the Subset wanted them together? Who knew and frankly, who cared? Elizabeth was tired of being a puppet of the Subset and living in fear and cowed obedience.

The results far exceeded her expectations. The wall blew outward, brick and mortar flying every which way. Liz and Elizabeth, now hand-in-hand, ducked to avoid flying debris. A shaft of light pierced its way through the large hole they'd made, revealing a hallway.

"Run!" Elizabeth screamed.

They both sprinted to the gaping hole and leapt through. The hallway was deserted but they could hear feet thundering overhead. They ran down the hallway, hesitated at the end, then instinctively turned left because the left forked to the longest hall, and started running again.

"Get them!" a voice yelled from another corridor. The whites of Liz's eyes reminded Elizabeth of a skittish mare, and she doubted she herself looked any different. Elizabeth was gasping now. Her sedentary lifestyle had not prepared her for explosive running. Liz, running like Zenyatta the mare, was having no such difficulty. She could easily have abandoned Elizabeth, but she stayed with her, dragging her by the hand. Two men in flak jackets appeared at the end of the corridor, holding guns trained on both women.

"Halt!" one of them screamed.

Liz didn't even slow down, just raised one hand and suddenly the men were blown backward, holes in their flak jackets as a force ripped straight through them, leaving an almost perfect circular hole in their midsections. As Elizabeth watched in horror, the intestines of one looped out lazily and fell to the ground.

"C'mon!" Liz screamed, and Elizabeth realized she'd slowed up almost instinctively. She started running again, making another left turn and heading down a new corridor. The corridor dead-ended and she and Liz both heard feet in the corridor they'd just left.

"Jesus Christ!" a voice yelled.

"I think they went that way," another voice hollered.

Liz and Elizabeth had almost reached the end of the corridor and now they raised their hands together and blew out the wall at the end. Sunlight streamed through. Outside was a grassy hillside. Without breaking stride, both women burst out and kept going, running parallel across the hillside toward the woods. Elizabeth had a stitch in her side and felt as if she would puke at any moment, but she forced herself onward. The woods were about four hundred yards away and sheltered. They reached it running full speed. As soon as they were safely in Elizabeth stepped behind a tree and began dry-heaving. Even her teeth hurt from the running. Her spit felt thick and there seemed to be too much of it for her mouth. She spat on the ground while Liz watched with a bemused look on her face.

"Damn, I'm the smoker, but you're really out of shape," she remarked.

"Shut up, kid," Elizabeth gasped. "I'm older. Are they coming?"

Liz looked back. "No."

Elizabeth was surprised. They'd gotten a head start, but if anyone had been in hot pursuit, they should have been in sight. This would all bear thinking about, but not right this second. Right now the best thing to do was just get as far away as possible. She began staggering, walking rapidly rather than running, into the deep woods. Liz walked alongside, keeping up as easily as if they'd been on a Sunday stroll. She made Elizabeth feel truly out of shape.

"Why do you think they aren't coming after us?" Liz asked after about ten minutes of walking. The trees were mostly evergreens, and for the most part they strolled on pine needles.

"Maybe," Elizabeth pointed out, "because you blew holes in two of their men. Jesus, how did you do that anyway?"

Liz shook her head, looking troubled. "I dunno. Trust me, I've never done that before. If I'd known I could do that, there's a lot of people I would have blown holes in before this."

A thoughtful and not especially nice look crossed her face. She looked as if she were picturing the people she could blow holes in, tasting the idea, and liking it very much. Inwardly, Elizabeth sighed. She was beginning to suspect that training Liz would consist of a lot more than just teaching her how to use her powers; it would also require teaching her when *not* to use them. And Liz was a pistol—literally. If she took it into her head to use her powers every time someone pissed her off, there would be a lot of dead people around soon. Which there already were, actually. That was part of the problem; people had a way of turning up dead when Liz was around.

"Use it sparingly," she confined herself to saying for now.

Liz was staring at the ground and didn't answer.

"Where are we going?" she asked finally, after a few more minutes of walking.

"Away from where we were," Elizabeth answered tersely. She'd been wondering that herself. She had no idea where they were, not even in which state. This could be as close as upstate New York, but depending upon how long they'd been unconscious, they could also have been shoved in a plane and be anywhere northern and green: Washington State, Oregon, Idaho. One guess was as good as another. She tried to think. It wasn't especially cold and for this time of year it should have been if they'd been in the northeast or the northwest. So maybe they were in Tennessee or South Carolina or even the mountains of New Mexico. She really had no idea. One step at a time was best for now, and the wisest course they could take was to get out of these woods and back to civilization.

"These woods freak me out," Liz said.

Elizabeth was surprised. Personally she loved the beauty and quiet of the woods. On the other hand, she'd grown up surrounded by them while Liz...

"You grew up in the city, didn't you?" she asked.

"Born and bred," Liz said proudly.

My sympathies, Elizabeth thought dryly.

"You're a country girl, aren't you?" commented Liz, who'd been watching from the corner of her eye.

"Born and bred," Elizabeth said, smiling a little.

Liz laughed. "City mouse, country mouse. So maybe you can tell me how we survive in these woods? Are there bears?"

"Bears don't bother you unless you bother them or you have food. If you get approached by a bear, just beat two sticks together. The noise scares them off. Same with other predators, like coyotes or wolves. But I've been running through woods my whole life and never been bothered by anything so I wouldn't worry about it."

"Oh but I do," Liz commented.

Elizabeth smiled but shook her head a little. She'd never get how people like Liz could live in cities, surrounded by lethal human animals, and yet think *bears* were dangerous. The only animal that had ever hurt Elizabeth was the human one, and she suspected that was true for Liz too.

City versus country, it didn't matter now. All that mattered was getting far away from the Subset. We did it, Elizabeth thought, the realization finally hitting her. We escaped from *them*! She laughed, twirling around, arms outstretched. Liz watched, looking amused, and that was fine, let her be amused; she'd never dealt with the Subset to the extent that Elizabeth had. She'd had only a taste of what they were capable of, while Elizabeth had been immersed in their world for years.

"We'll head due west," she said.

"How do you know which way we're going?" Liz asked.

"By the sun," Elizabeth answered. "And when it gets dark, I'll use the north star to keep us on track."

"I love people who can do that shit," Liz said.

"Thanks," Elizabeth said.

They walked mostly in silence for a few hours. The tranquility of the woods should have made Elizabeth feel better but didn't. She didn't know what the Subset was up to now, but she did know that there was no way they would just accept the killing of two of their men and allow Liz and Elizabeth to disappear forever after they'd invested God knows how much in capturing them for whatever purpose. The fact that no one had come after them yet made Elizabeth more nervous. It meant they were planning something more elaborate than men with guns or dogs that Liz could and would blow to bits. Perhaps they'd come up with something that Liz couldn't fight. But what would it be? And how could they know when Liz and Elizabeth had been unaware of the full extent of their powers together until they'd used them this morning?

Shortly after sunset Elizabeth had to concede defeat. Her powers did not extend to letting her see in the dark, and she was constantly stumbling.

"We should stop and sleep now," she said, hoping Liz wouldn't object.

Liz was almost breathing down her neck—she'd been sticking very close ever since the sun set. "Okay," she said cheerfully.

They settled in under a tree, side by side on the pine needles. It was a bit lumpier than Elizabeth would have liked but she hardly had a choice.

"Good night," she said to Liz.

Liz didn't answer, instead rolling over and wrapping her arms around Elizabeth, snuggling against her. It was a very presumptuous move, almost clingy, and made Elizabeth uncomfortable. "Good night," Liz finally murmured.

Elizabeth didn't move for the next half hour. Having Liz so close made her nervous, but a small part of her also enjoyed it. The girl was little and cute, and sometimes…not often but sometimes…it was just nice to have human contact. However, she would have liked to choose when she'd have that human contact. Though admittedly if anyone waited for her to make the first move, even in a casual friendship, they might be waiting a damn long time. So maybe Liz wasn't being presumptuous but just more forward than Elizabeth would have been. They lay there in silence for about half an hour, then Liz began stroking Elizabeth's arm and slipped one hand under her sweatshirt, touching her skin on the side of her abdomen. Again, those hands, unbelievably warm. Elizabeth swallowed, suddenly feeling self-conscious about what she perceived as her fat stomach. Tiny as she was, what must Liz think of it? Then she felt angry with herself for even worrying about it in the first place. What did it matter what Liz thought of her body? The point was, did she even want Liz touching her in the first place?

Yes.

No. Okay, maybe part of her did but overall…not a good idea, no matter how nice it felt, no matter how cute Liz was and how nice she could be. Elizabeth had still barely scratched the surface of getting to know Liz, and she knew there were a lot of demons lurking below the surface, and demons had a way of emerging with intimacy. Better to keep her distance. Liz was still stroking her side and now moved her hand up toward Elizabeth's breasts. Elizabeth quickly grabbed her wrist and moved it back down and away from her.

"What are you doing?" she asked gently.

"Don't you like it?" Liz asked, sounding anxious.

How to answer that? Yes, I like it but I still don't think it's a good idea? No, I don't like it because it may feel good but you're still crazier than a cuckoo bird?

"It feels nice," she said aloud, "but I don't think it's a good idea."

"Why not?"

"I don't want to be involved with you that way."

Liz laughed, sounding relieved. "Oh, it doesn't *mean* anything. It's not like we're dating or something. I just thought it would feel nice."

"To me it does mean something," Elizabeth said firmly. Call me old-fashioned, she thought, call me whatever; being touched was an intense experience and it would change the dynamics of her relationship with Liz in a way she didn't think she'd like.

"Oh." Liz sounded a bit more subdued now. "I'm sorry. I just thought—it was dark and I don't want to be alone, and I thought if we had sex, it would feel nice. You don't have to reciprocate or anything, I can just do everything."

Elizabeth laughed in spite of herself, in spite of the awkwardness. "I don't suck *that* much in bed," she said. "I'm happy to reciprocate when the time and place and person is right. This just…isn't it."

"Oh." Liz rolled away so she was no longer touching Elizabeth. "I'm sorry."

"Are you mad at me?" Elizabeth asked, feeling slightly incredulous and ready to be angry herself. To think of someone getting mad just because she wouldn't let them sleep with her was absurd.

"Not mad," Liz said, after a few moments in a tiny voice. "Just embarrassed."

"Why?" Elizabeth asked.

"You don't want me."

"It has nothing to do with wanting you or not wanting you. It has nothing to do with you at all. It has to do with me and with what I want, what being touched means to me. You *are* very cute, you know."

"Really?" Liz sounded a little cheered up.

"Yes, really."

Liz was quiet for a few minutes. An owl hooted in the distance. Elizabeth shifted on the pine needles, ready to go to sleep.

"Can we still cuddle?" Liz asked hesitantly.

"Of course."

Liz quickly scooted back over to her. Elizabeth rolled over and wrapped her arms protectively around the tinier woman.

"Thank you," Liz said softly.

"Not a problem. It's even…sort of a pleasure."

Liz smiled in the darkness, taking hold of Elizabeth's hand, and gradually they fell asleep, breathing in sync, curled up closely together.

CHAPTER SIX

The next morning Elizabeth woke before the sun rose and quickly shook Liz awake. She felt stiff and was damp with dew. The morning air was cold and humid. She caught a fetid whiff from the sweatsuit she was still wearing. They were past due for a bath.

"C'mon," she said. "We have to get moving."

Liz quickly stood up, not questioning her urgency. Both of them could sense that something had happened in the night while they slept. Forces had been set in motion and now there would be people after them. From far away, Elizabeth fancied she could hear a hound baying but whether it was just in her imagination or even had anything to do with her, she didn't know.

"I'm thirsty," Liz commented.

"Grab some leaves," Elizabeth said. "There should be dew in them, and you can drink that. It's not much, but it's better than nothing."

Liz obediently began gathering leaves, licking off the dew, and Elizabeth followed suit. She wasn't especially thirsty yet, but she knew that she would be later, and later would be too late when the sun had dried everything. They spent about ten minutes drinking dew and then were on their way again, heading west.

"So what's the plan?" Liz asked, falling into step slightly behind Elizabeth.

"I'm hoping we hit a town soon," Elizabeth admitted. "When we do that, we stand a chance of getting away. You don't know how to hot-wire a car, do you?"

"Of course," Liz said casually as if such things were common knowledge that everyone should know.

"Seriously?"

"Yeah."

Elizabeth's spirits lifted. "That's perfect then! We hot-wire a car and then get the hell out of here. Once that's done, we can plan our next step."

"Okay," Liz said. "Out of curiosity, what made you choose west anyway?"

"Because it's completely random," Elizabeth admitted. "If we plan based on a strategy then I guarantee you there is someone in the Subset who can anticipate us, outsmart us and be waiting for us. But if our moves are completely random, there's no anticipating, no outthinking. They can't account for the random. No one can. That's the best thing we have going for us."

"Cool," Liz said.

They walked through most of the morning as the sun gradually came up, dissipating the fog on the forest floor, then rising over the trees in a red blaze, creeping through the sky, turning the air from cool and moist to hot and humid. Liz slipped off her sweatshirt and tied it around her waist, leaving on only her bra. That struck Elizabeth as one of the most sensible things she'd seen all morning, and she quickly followed suit, enjoying the feel of the air kissing her sweaty skin and gently cooling it.

"You have awesome breasts," Liz commented, smirking a little.

Elizabeth, who'd at one point been self-conscious about her 36DD bra size was beginning to get a handle on Liz's sense of humor and didn't let it faze her. "I'm sure you do too," she said. "Once someone finds them."

Liz laughed aloud, appreciatively. "Oooh, snap! Bi-atch." She raised one foot behind her and lightly kicked Elizabeth on the butt.

Elizabeth kicked her back. "Douche bag."

They walked in companionable silence for another ten minutes till they came to a slight rise. On the other side of it and below them was a small town. It looked like a toy town from up where they were, all white houses, buildings with red bricks, and churches with steeples. Liz and Elizabeth both stopped and stared.

"Mecca," Liz breathed.

She started forward and Elizabeth quickly put a restraining hand on her arm. "Wait," she said. "We can't be seen."

"Why not? You don't think they're down there, do you?"

"Of course they are. And if by some chance they aren't yet, they will be later and they'll be asking questions about two women humping it across country in matching sweatsuits. It's just better that we're not seen."

"Makes sense," Liz agreed. "So what do you propose we do?"

"Head down cautiously and keep a low profile. It's about all we can do."

Liz nodded.

They pulled their sweatshirts back on and, carefully, they began picking their way down the hill toward the town, making sure to keep behind bushes whenever possible. Finally they reached the bottom of the hill and peeked out toward the main street. It wasn't crowded, but there were enough people around that neither woman felt comfortable venturing out to scope out and steal a car.

"C'mon," Elizabeth whispered. "We'll stick here in the woods and creep around to see if we can find the residential area. That should be less visible."

They crept through the woods, along Main Street which then led up a hill and gradually the few small businesses disappeared, and there was just a smattering of houses here and there, looking dilapidated and in need of paint. In front of one of them was an orange VW Bug. Elizabeth stopped and nudged Liz.

"Do you think you could get that one?" she asked.

Liz nodded. "Yeah. The older models are easier. They have safeguards on the new ones that I haven't figured out yet. But that one should be fine."

They both crouched down and watched the house for about ten minutes. There was no sign of movement from inside or around the outside. The neighboring townhouses were quiet too.

"I think this is as good as it gets," Elizabeth said finally.

Liz nodded. "Okay. Let's do it. Walk don't run though."

As if Elizabeth needed to be told. They walked across the street, trying not to appear conspicuous. When they reached the Bug, Liz tried the door and was in luck. She grinned across the roof at Elizabeth who quickly opened the passenger side and slipped in as Liz did the same on her side. Elizabeth waited in agony as Liz fiddled with wires under the steering column. She could feel sweat breaking out on her back underneath her bra. Liz seemed to take forever. But then the engine roared to life, and Liz turned to her, giving her a triumphant smile. Elizabeth couldn't help smiling back and holding up her hand for a high five.

"Life of crime pays off," she said, then wondered if she'd actually said that aloud, but Liz just laughed appreciatively as she backed carefully out of the driveway and onto the street.

"Now what?" Liz asked.

"Head south," Elizabeth said automatically.

Liz didn't question why, just headed south without needing to ask which way that was. She'd picked up on reading the sun for directions.

"We have a little over half a tank," she said, "which should take us a good distance. These Bugs get good mileage." She patted the dashboard fondly.

Elizabeth made her lips curve upward in a facsimile of a smile, but inwardly her mind was whirring and churning, trying to think of what would need to come next. Money. Food. Shelter. They needed all those things. Really, the bottom line was, how long could they evade the Subset? They were not hiding now; they were running. And how long and how far could they run? The world was round; eventually they'd come back to where they started.

One thing at a time, Elizabeth promised herself. And it occurred to her that she had a great resource at hand, perhaps the greatest resource she could ever have asked for: Liz. A woman who held no regular job but somehow always managed to eat, if not well, and keep a roof over her head. A character from the fringe. And the fringe was the safest place to hide from the Subset, the fringe where the forgotten and the disappeared of society dwelled. Deep down, Elizabeth had always longed to drop out of society and find something else, carve her own meaning and write her own words, her own history. For better or for worse, she suspected she was about to get that chance now.

"We have no money," she said aloud.

As she'd expected, Liz just shrugged. "We don't need that stuff," she said.

"Where do you think we should stay?" Elizabeth asked.

Again, a shrug. "Anywhere. The shelters would be cool. They ask for a name but if you got no ID, you can just make one up."

Of course. Shelters. Soup kitchens. All places where someone could hunker down and lay low. Elizabeth stared at Liz gratefully and with new respect. "You rock," she said.

"I know," Liz said matter-of-factly.

* * *

Twelve hours later, Elizabeth was not so sure of that. She was sleeping in the backseat of a '78 Chevette in a Walmart parking lot. Liz was snoozing in the front seat. They'd found the car at a McDonald's when the gas in the Bug had started getting low. They'd boosted the car with no trouble and had even managed to figure out what state they were in by license plates on the road and seeing the newspapers: Tennessee.

Elizabeth knew jack about Tennessee, and Liz knew even less. Liz had taught Elizabeth about table diving at McDonald's: waiting until customers finished and left their trays of often half-eaten meals on the table. Then swoop down and eat what was left. It wasn't gourmet dining, but it was food and it succeeded in taking away the hunger pangs. After a while, the manager started giving them the stink-eye and finally came over and asked them pointblank if they had any plans to order anything.

"Hell no," Liz said coolly, grabbing a half a soda off a table and pushing past him. Feeling embarrassed and yet somehow proud of Liz, Elizabeth followed. They'd gone out to the street, walked around the block, then back to the McDonald's parking lot where Liz boosted the car. "I hope to Christ it belongs to that manager," she commented as they pulled out.

Elizabeth just giggled, feeling very much out of her element here.

They drove for about four more hours and then the gas started getting low again. Liz abruptly pulled into a Walmart parking lot. "We'll sleep here," she announced. "Walmart is cool. They let you sleep in the parking lot as long as you stay near the back and don't bother anyone."

Elizabeth didn't bother to ask how Liz had come by this handy-dandy piece of information. She was just glad that somehow she had.

In the dark, lying in the backseat, she began to feel oddly exhilarated.

So this is what freedom is like.

It was grubby and hard, and materially she had absolutely nothing to call her own. Everything she got from now on would have to be begged for, borrowed or stolen, but she did have one thing: herself. For the first time since childhood.

In the morning, they went inside to use the bathroom and wash up. Liz also stole a can of Chef Boyardee ravioli with a pull-top lid. They ate in the car with their fingers, passing the can back and forth until it was empty. Elizabeth could feel that her sweatpants, grubby as they might be, were also fitting a bit looser.

"We're going to need more clothes," she said, wondering where Liz might know of to take care of that.

Liz didn't disappoint. Licking ravioli off her fingers, she just nodded.

"We'll swipe another car," she said, "go until the gas runs out and then hit up a church. Most of them have free food and clothes, and if they don't, they'll know where we can get some. I used to get all my clothes and food from the church."

"Are you…a Christian?" Elizabeth asked.

Liz laughed so hard a piece of ravioli flew out her nose. When she finally got herself together, she managed to shake her head. "I'm a godless heathen, honey, you should know that. But on occasion, I've *wished* I was religious. If that makes any sense."

Elizabeth nodded. Considering the amount of free stuff Liz was racking up from the churches, she could understand why she'd have some appreciation for them. Elizabeth herself had never had any use for organized religion, but she'd also never been truly hungry or destitute before and then taken care of by a church.

A car pulled in behind them. A black Town Car with tinted windows. Another pulled in to the right of them and then a third pulled over on the left side. Black Lincoln Town Cars with tinted windows: it was such a cliché that Elizabeth knew it could only be the Subset. They used clichés, not in spite of the fact that they were clichés but because they were, for the power they had to induce universal terror and it never failed to work.

Liz caught on quick. She leapt out of the car and started running. Two men came out of the Town Car behind them and fired a tranquilizer gun at her. She went down without a sound. Elizabeth heard her door being opened, started to turn and felt a sharp prick in her neck. Then there was only darkness.

* * *

Elizabeth woke up naked lying on a metal table in a lead-lined room with white walls and one steel door. It was a tiny room, about the size of a doctor's office. The only furniture, apart from the table, was a small wooden chair. Fluorescent lights overhead burned down on her.

The steel door slid open with a small whooshing sound and a man in a gray suit stepped inside. He was lean and fit, somewhere in his late forties or early fifties, with salt-and-pepper hair and wire-rimmed spectacles. He sat in the chair near the table. Feeling completely unself-conscious about being nude, Elizabeth sat up and swung her legs over the table's edge, facing him. She had a strange relationship with her body. They'd been through so much together that she no longer felt any shame about it. It was hers, it would always be hers, no one could take that away, and she didn't care who saw it. The man did not seem interested in the fact that she was nude either.

"You're awake," he said mildly.

"Yes."

Long silence. The man seemed to be thinking. Elizabeth waited.

He asked, "Can you tell us how you and the girl Liz came to have the same frequency, and how you pulled off the stunt you did the other day?"

"No."

"No, you can't tell us or no, you won't tell us?"

"Can't tell you."

The man nodded. "People are not happy with you. At the same time…we've never seen a demonstration of power like that. At least not at your level. Your abilities were tested years ago. There is no way you should have been able to do what you did. Nor should Liz. But you did it."

"Yes."

Another long silence.

"Very well. I'll be back." He stood up.

"Can I have clothes?"

"No." He left.

Elizabeth continued to sit patiently on the edge of the table, letting her mind wander, trying to find Liz.

* * *

Liz had none of Elizabeth's equanimity. She woke up naked on the table in an identical room to the one Elizabeth was in, but her reaction was very different. She immediately pulled her legs up to her chest, wrapping her arms protectively around her knees and effectively covering herself while glancing around fiercely. Then she leapt off the table and ran to the door, pushing against it, trying to slide it open. She picked up the wooden chair and slammed it against the door until the chair broke in two. The door remained unmarked.

"Lemme outta here!" she screamed. "You fuckers! I'll kill you!" She beat against the door with her fists, not really expecting anything to happen but too stubborn to simply sit and wait.

The door abruptly slid open; a man in a gray suit entered. She took a step back. Behind the man, she could see two other men in uniforms and helmets, holding guns, waiting at attention. Then the door slid shut and hid them from view.

"Hello, Liz," the man said, looking at the broken chair on the floor. He seemed amused which just pissed Liz off.

"Who're you?" she snapped.

"Someone with a great deal of interest in you."

"Where's Elizabeth?"

"She's fine."

"What do you want with me?"

The man leaned against the wall, folding his arms thoughtfully. "We want to know how you did what you did to escape," he said.

Liz moved to the other side of the table where she was blocked from his view and felt slightly less exposed. "I don't know." She tried mentally to blow a hole in his chest. Without Elizabeth though, it was no good. She could do nothing.

The man rubbed his chin, pursed his lips and looked at the floor. "I was afraid of that," he said, straightening up. "Well, no matter. We'll figure it out eventually."

He left. Quickly, before Liz even had a chance to realize what he was doing. As the door slid shut behind him, she ran over and grabbed at it, her fingers slipping on the metal.

"You fucker!" she screamed. "Let me out!"

* * *

"Charming, isn't she?" said John Peters. He was an older man in his late fifties, stout, with a mole on the left side of his nose that quivered when he was angry. Right now it was still. He looked amused. He wore a gray suit as did the younger man next to him. They were in a small dark room filled with monitors, all showing Liz and Elizabeth from different angles.

A younger man with empty brown eyes, Byron Todd allowed himself a chuckle then spoke. "What I still want to know," he said, "is how she could have the same frequency as Elizabeth. You know the odds of that. It's like fingerprints. She *can't* have it..."

"But she does. I know. And it gets twice as strong when they're together."

"It makes no sense."

"Then we test them until it does. There's always an answer."

Byron nodded thoughtfully, brow furrowed, accepting the truth of this statement, and they both turned their attention to the cameras and the two very different women in different rooms. Byron did not like mysteries, but he liked challenges, and these women, he suspected, would be worthy of whatever he could throw at them. He thought that might be fun, to see how much they could endure.

* * *

Liz tried to blow out the wall the way she had the first time they'd escaped. She extended her hand, concentrated her energy, tried to fire it. She was tapped out. She could feel it inside. She just didn't know why. When she'd been with Elizabeth it had been as if there were an endless supply of energy. They'd seemed to feed off each other, and there had been nothing they couldn't do.

Liz tried to find Elizabeth with her mind. She concentrated very hard and gradually she was able to pick up a room similar to the one she was in. But she had no idea where that room was or how to get there or even how to get out of the room she was in. As much as she hated to admit it, the best and only thing to do was wait.

She sat down on the edge of the table and waited. She shivered, wishing they'd bring her a hospital gown or something to cover her. The room was not chilly, but when you were buck naked, anything made you feel cold.

In Elizabeth's room, she was also waiting patiently and visualizing herself on a warm desert island so she wasn't cold. On the island, she had a piña colada in one hand and a Stephen King book in the other. Life was paradise.

In their little room, high above the theater, the men watched the two women on camera. Every now and then other people would wander through their lookout, watch for a while and then leave. Liz and Elizabeth were hot news in the compound, but today was a slow day, with no outward action from the women. Everyone gradually relaxed. If either woman could do something on her own proportionate to what they'd done together, it was being hidden well. No, their magic happened when they were together, and there was still the matter of the matching frequencies and brain waves. Nobody could explain that. They wanted and needed to, urgently.

"What do we do now?" Peters finally asked.

Byron shrugged. He took out a cigarette and lit it carefully, knowing it bothered the older man and also knowing Peters wouldn't dare say anything. Indeed, the irritation factor of his cigarette was one of the few reasons he still smoked despite getting no real pleasure from the act. He liked needling people, getting under their skin and seeing how far he could push. Only after he'd performed his ritual with the cigarette did he speak again.

"We let them go," he said. "Let them go, trace them, and see what they do. Especially…especially if we put them in danger."

"They'll never buy that! Well, the younger one might, but not Elizabeth. She's been around too long, she'd know something was up."

"This time they escape with no pursuit so there's no casualties. Then we simply follow using Elizabeth's imbedded tracking device."

"What if they split up?"

A puff on the cigarette before answering. "They won't."

"How do you know?"

"Because they need each other."

Peters frowned. He did not like or trust Byron who had the soul of a piranha but the man was seldom wrong. "All right."

* * *

After another six hours of the two women waiting, uniformed men came separately but at the same time, to escort Elizabeth and Liz out of their waiting rooms and down to the cafeteria. They were carrying sweatsuits and tossed one to each woman.

Elizabeth pulled hers on. No underwear or bra and it was a little too tight, but it was better than being naked. A pair of size seven sneakers fortunately fit just right.

Liz found hers a little too large, including the sneakers. She put everything on without complaint and let the man take her by the arm and guide her out. He was holding a rifle which made her much less inclined to get feisty.

Liz was guided down a hallway, around a corner, and into a cafeteria. The cafeteria was empty except for a woman in a gray sweatsuit seated at a long table down at the far end, the last table in a row of seven that filled the cafeteria. The woman had long blond hair. She looked like…

"Elizabeth!" Liz yelled, breaking away from her guard and running toward her.

Elizabeth stood up. She had an untouched tray of food in front of her. Liz ran into her arms and they embraced.

Liz stroked Elizabeth's hair. "You're safe!"

"So are you."

One of the men cleared his throat finally. "This is beautiful, but if you wanna eat, I suggest you go get your tray."

He gestured toward the side of the cafeteria where there was a small door leading into a kitchen. Liz dutifully headed over and went inside. There was a stack of trays and a buffet-style cafeteria line of food. None of it looked especially appetizing, but it wasn't bad either. The kitchen was untended so she helped herself, and then went back to the main part of the cafeteria. Elizabeth was still sitting at the far table in the corner, her food untouched. The two men who'd escorted them were gone.

"Where did the goons go?" Liz asked, sitting down next to her.

"I dunno," Elizabeth said, sounding unhappy.

Liz was shocked by her demeanor. "Don't tell me you're sorry to see them go!"

"Not sorry. I just…don't like it. Something's not right. Look at that." She picked up her fork and gestured toward the far side of the cafeteria. A metal door was propped open. Outside a bit of a parking lot and the sky could be seen.

Outside?

Liz also immediately felt a sense of misgiving but quashed it. "We can escape," she whispered loudly, smiling.

Elizabeth shook her head. "It's not escape when they let you go," she said in a low voice.

"But maybe it's a mistake. They just forgot it."

"The Subset doesn't forget anything."

Liz felt a surge of irritation. "You talk as if they're all-powerful and all-knowing. You forget we did escape from them once. So they're not perfect."

She was afraid Elizabeth might be angry at her, but Elizabeth just looked even more thoughtful. "That's just it. We did escape from them once. They'd never let it happen again. Unless they wanted it to." She took a bite of food.

Liz stared at her in disbelief then swatted her fork away. It flew across the table and clanged loudly on the floor, bouncing several feet. "I can't believe you're fucking sitting here and eating. Let's go!" She stood up.

Elizabeth hesitated then reluctantly stood up as well.

"We're being played with," she said unhappily, and into her head, unbidden, came the image of ants under a dome, running about, thinking they were free, while above them, unseen, observers controlled the whole environment, watching them with clinical interest.

Still, they'd been left with no other logical move. She felt as she were being forced into the losing end of a game, checkmated against her will, but what choice was there? She and Liz walked over to the door. Despite knowing they were intended to do this, she still half expected someone to come rushing in and stop them at the last minute.

They walked out into a sunny parking lot in a residential neighborhood. There was a smattering of about six ordinary looking cars in the lot. Beyond that was a string of small pleasant-looking houses. On the other side, the parking lot dipped down into a culvert and some woods.

Even Liz looked uncertain. "Which way should we go?" she whispered as if someone could still hear them.

Elizabeth shrugged. "If they want us back, they'll come get us. I say we take the most comfortable route." She headed across the parking lot for the sidewalk in front of the houses.

Liz hesitated then followed her. Glancing at Elizabeth, she noticed that her face looked troubled. Their hands bumped together, and she instinctively took Elizabeth's hand for comfort, not thinking of how it might look to onlookers to see two grown women in matching sweatsuits walking hand-in-hand down the sidewalk of a small and what looked like a decidedly conservative town. Fortunately Elizabeth didn't seem to mind.

"What's wrong?" Liz asked.

Elizabeth removed her hand from Liz's—immediately Liz missed the warmth of it—and made a fist and thumped it against the open palm of her other hand.

"It's how they found us," she said. "Aghh! I can't figure it out. We did everything right. They should not have known where we were."

"But they did," Liz said, shrugging as she felt the warm sun beating through her sweatsuit and onto her shoulders.

"But how?" Elizabeth complained. "How could they have done it?"

"Maybe they put a microscopic tracking device in our clothes. Or our hair."

Elizabeth shook her head. "Too much chance of it getting lost or ruined when we washed. Which eventually we would have done," she added with a faint smile.

Liz shrugged again. She'd seen enough movies to know that it was easy. "So maybe they implanted it under our skin," she tossed out casually as if such things were common occurrences.

Elizabeth abruptly stopped walking. Liz took two steps further before realizing Elizabeth was no longer with her.

"What now?" she asked impatiently, anxious to be getting on their way.

Elizabeth had a slightly mad look in her eyes. She grabbed the sleeve of her sweatshirt and yanked it up, then held out her arm, revealing the smooth underside of her forearm. "What do you see?" she demanded.

In the center of the arm was a very conspicuous scar, about three inches long and a quarter of an inch wide. It was an old scar and white and keloid tissue had formed over it. "It looks like you cut yourself," Liz said.

Elizabeth shook her head. "I didn't do it. It's been there since…my days in the military. I never quite remembered how I got it, and the funny thing is that it didn't even seem odd at the time. I always scarred and bruised easy so I thought it was just another unexplained scratch."

"Yeah, but that's a big one," Liz pointed out.

"Well, no shit. Maybe they hypnotized me. Anyway, I'm wondering. Maybe…what if they put a tracking device in *me*? Then they could find us whenever they wanted."

Liz eyeballed the scar on Elizabeth's arm with some skepticism. In spite of everything they'd been through, seen and done, she still couldn't get used to the idea that people like this actually existed and did these kinds of things. "So how are we supposed to know for sure?" she asked.

Elizabeth grimaced. Her face had begun to look very pale. "There is only one way," she said.

Liz could think of only thing, and surely Elizabeth didn't mean *that*. "What?" she asked aloud.

Elizabeth did mean *that*. "You have to cut it open and see if there's a device," she said.

Liz was already shaking her head. "Oh no. That's crazy talk. I'm not doing anything like that. What if you're wrong?"

"Then I'm wrong, and I end up with a boo-boo, and we buy some Band-Aids. But if I'm right, then this could make the difference between being under their eye and thumb constantly or actually having a chance at freedom."

Liz bit her lip, but already she knew that Elizabeth was right. It made sense, damn it. "Fine," she said. "But then we get some new clothes and some food, and we take it easy for a night. Deal?" She was insistent on this last part. Elizabeth didn't look so good; she had dark circles under her eyes and her skin looked gray and washed out.

Elizabeth nodded. "Fair enough."

"So how did you expect to do this?" Liz asked, still holding Elizabeth's wrist and looking at the scar again. "Have me rip it open with my teeth and root around in there while we stand here?"

"No. I was sort of, well, hoping you could steal some razor blades and we could go into the woods or something," Elizabeth mumbled, not meeting Liz's eyes.

Liz scowled. "Why am *I* stealing the razor blades?"

"Because you're better at it than me."

"What makes you assume that?"

"I just...I never do it so I thought..."

"So you thought I did because naturally I'd be a thief, and what's it matter if I get caught, right?"

"Look, I'm sorry, I didn't mean it like that. I'll steal the stupid—"

Liz laughed. "Ah, don't worry about it. I'm just messin' with you. Of course, I'll steal 'em. Milquetoast like you would get your ass caught in a heartbeat."

"I'll have you know I had my own wild streak back in the day," Elizabeth said, smiling a little.

Liz slapped her lightly on the shoulder. "Well, that day was a long time ago because now you reek of yuppie. C'mon, let's find a store," she added, before Elizabeth could come up with a rejoinder for that last crack.

They ambled down the sidewalk for a couple of miles and eventually reached the outskirts of the town where sure enough, there was a great big ugly Walmart. "Perfect," Liz said. "You wait out here." She tapped Elizabeth lightly on the shoulder then disappeared into the store.

Elizabeth leaned against an empty bike rack, sweating in the sun and eyeballing the water machine wistfully. Her mouth felt as if it were stuffed full of cotton. She waited for what seemed like hours and was about to head inside when Liz exited the store with a rolling gait, took Elizabeth's arm and guided her back down the sidewalk.

"Did you get it?" Elizabeth asked. "I was starting to get worried."

"No worries, mate," Liz said cheerfully in a fake Aussie accent.

She seemed very chipper, and it occurred to Elizabeth that Liz always seemed chipper when they were on the run and stealing stuff. Peace seemed to be her worst enemy—she thrived on chaos. Well, that was good because there was plenty of chaos to go around right now. Liz was about to get all she could handle. "I got the razor blades, some tweezers and also some butterfly bandages and gauze and antiseptic so we can fix you up after," Liz added.

"Where is it?" Elizabeth asked.

"Stuffed down the front of my pants," Liz said.

Elizabeth looked over from the corners of her eyes as they made their way down the sidewalk, and sure enough she could just faintly see that the bottom of Liz's right leg, above the elastic at the ankle of the sweats, was bulging slightly. She smiled in spite of herself.

"Your criminal tendencies are coming in very handy," she said.

Liz looked delighted. "Stick with me, doll, and you'll never go hungry again."

Elizabeth laughed despite faint misgivings. All this banter and what was basically a light type of flirting was well and fine, but she hoped Liz understood that it was just a friendly thing and would never be going any further.

Why not?

There were a lot of reasons. Namely that she had her own baggage and delightful as Liz could be when she was in good spirits, Elizabeth hadn't forgotten that she also had a dark and very troubled side, and troubled was putting it mildly and nicely.

"Never say never," Liz sang, abruptly breaking into what Elizabeth recognized as an old Romeo Void tune from the eighties.

"You weren't even born when that song came out," she joked.

"So what?" Liz said in mock indignation.

"How old *are* you anyway?"

"Twenty-four."

Twenty-four. So only twelve years younger than Elizabeth, not so young as she'd feared, not too young to rule out a relationship but still…no. Just no. Though stranger things had happened, she supposed. Initially, she had disliked this girl before ever even meeting her, and now…what did she feel now? Fond of her certainly, and she would even consider her a friend. But not romance potential. Not that it even mattered much. Romance was the last thing she needed to be worrying about now. Getting her life back and escaping her fate as a tool of the Subset was enough to worry about.

"Hush with the singing," she said, nudging Liz's arm. Liz had just broken into another refrain. "You're drawing attention to us."

"I like attention," Liz said, but obediently shut up.

They walked until they were back in the residential area, and there was a park behind a library with some woods surrounding it.

"We'll do it over there," Elizabeth said firmly.

Liz looked more serious now, her jocularity gone. "Are you sure about this?" she asked.

"I'm sure," Elizabeth said. "We don't have a choice."

They walked through the park and deep into the woods. Elizabeth went behind a clump of bushes and removed her sweatshirt. Liz, her sneakered feet crunching on dry leaves, crouched next to her as Elizabeth held out her arm. Elizabeth was completely naked from the waist up, but for once Liz made no jokes about her breasts. She looked a bit pale as she studied the arm. She stretched out her right leg, lifted the elastic by her ankle and pulled out the packages of razor blades, tweezers, a small bottle of antiseptic, bandages and gauze. Carefully, she laid them on the ground then ripped open the razor blades and the tweezers, being sure to set the tweezers on the cardboard packaging rather than in the dirt.

"You sure about this?" she asked curtly.

Elizabeth nodded and held out her arm, balancing it against her own leg, turning her face away. Liz took out one of the razor blades, poured antiseptic over it and then took hold of Elizabeth's arm firmly enough to be distractingly painful and, holding the arm steady with her right hand, cut into it deftly along the scar. The arm opened up like butter. She had cut into the subcutaneous layer which was almost all fat. She picked up the tweezers and gently nudged the layers of skin aside.

"I don't see—wait." She pushed the skin aside a little more. "Holy shit!"

Elizabeth released the breath she was holding against the pain.

"Do you see something?" she asked, trying to peek. Liz was bent over her arm and her head was blocking Elizabeth's view.

"Yeah. I think so. Hold on."

Her tongue poking out slightly, she grasped the tweezers firmly and reached inside, taking hold of something and yanked.

The pain was so sharp and severe that Elizabeth sucked in a deep breath to keep from screaming.

"There!" Liz said triumphantly.

Shimmering in blood that reflected in an almost metallic way against the afternoon sunlight through the trees was an object approximately an inch and a half long and a quarter of an inch wide. It looked like an elongated microchip.

"Motherfuck," Elizabeth said.

That was inside of me. Monitoring me all these years, doing God knows what else.

She fainted.

Liz stared in surprise. The unflappable Elizabeth had... flapped. Though if she herself had found some strange device in her arm, she might have fainted too. It was one thing to think such things were possible; it was another to realize they were not only possible, but that all your most paranoid fantasies were real. She quickly opened the bandages and gauze, dabbed away the blood on Elizabeth's arm, poured antiseptic on the entire area, put the butterfly bandages on to close the wound and then wrapped gauze around it, taping it in place at the end with two more bandages. Then she lightly slapped Elizabeth's cheek.

"Wake up, sister. Nappy time is over."

Elizabeth moaned and her eyes blinked open. "What the hell," she murmured. She sat up slowly then looked down at her throbbing arm and shuddered. "Is it...gone?"

Liz nodded at the cardboard box on the ground that had held the tweezers. They were resting there now, along with the device. Elizabeth grimaced as she picked up her sweatshirt and slowly pulled it back on, careful not to dislodge the fresh bandage.

"That was disgusting," she said. The pain in her arm was intense.

"Put me right in the mood for a steak," Liz joked.

Elizabeth didn't answer. For once she wasn't in the mood for Liz's jokes.

Liz seemed to sense that a moment too late and put an apologetic hand on Elizabeth's shoulder. "I'm sorry," she said. "You doing okay?"

"Yeah. I will be anyway. Thanks for—for getting that *thing* out of me."

"Not a problem." Liz scooped up all the supplies from the ground. "What should we do with it all?"

A slow grin spread over Elizabeth's face. "I've got an idea," she said, standing up and brushing the leaves and twigs off her pants. "Follow me." The pain in her arm was beginning to subside.

A few minutes later, two women in sweatshirts could be seen in the library parking lot. They paused by the rear of a car then one squatted down and shoved something behind the license plate. They stood up and walked away quickly, unobserved.

"That'll fool 'em for a few days anyway," Elizabeth said. "So long as the device is occasionally moving, they'll assume it's still in me, and when it's not moving, hopefully they figure I'm sleeping."

"I hope so," Liz said, though she already had her doubts. If anyone was watching in person, even from a distance, it wouldn't take them long to realize they were observing a car rather than Elizabeth. Still, even a day or two of a head start could be invaluable. "Come on," she said. "Let's find a church, and I'll show you how to get free clothes and food."

They hurried away.

CHAPTER SEVEN

Just as Liz had predicted, they found a church that gave them free clothes and some food, and two days later, after hitchhiking their way, they were sleeping in a shelter in Florida, and debating how to get some permanent identification.

"Right now, we're still running," Elizabeth whispered.

It was about two in the morning and the other women in the cots around them were either asleep or too far away to worry about, but nonetheless Elizabeth *did* worry. She'd seen firsthand what the Subset could do and it would not do to lose any respect for them. She'd been lucky so far, but this was just a beginning.

In the back of her mind, she knew this couldn't go on forever. It *could*, but she didn't *want* it to. She did not want to spend the rest of her life on the run. Which left only one option: stand her ground and fight. But how did you fight an organization that was so large and nebulous you could barely see them? It was like trying to wrestle smoke. It was nearly impossible.

"So what of it?" said Liz, who was far more comfortable with running. "As long as we stay ahead of the bastards, what's to worry about? We go about our thing and never have to see them again."

"And what's your thing?" Elizabeth asked warily, knowing full well what Liz's "thing" had been, at least prior to meeting Elizabeth. Perhaps that explained the cold look Liz gave her and the icy response. Or maybe the hour was just late and they were both tired.

"It's none of your fucking business, is it?"

Elizabeth recoiled in spite of herself. She'd gotten used to cheerful, cuddly, teddy-bear Liz who joked and was so considerate; she'd forgotten about this other Liz that lurked below the surface. But now, staring into those dark eyes which had grown impenetrable, she was forcefully reminded that Liz wasn't remotely like all the other girls.

"No need to be a bitch," she murmured.

"Oh yes there is. I'm the most cold-blooded bitch you'll ever meet and don't forget it," Liz said, her voice still low and utterly lacking in all warmth or tone.

"Yeah, well…we're in this together."

Liz seemed to relax a little at this. She'd been sitting rigidly on her cot, legs crossed in the center of an itchy gray woolen blanket, and now her shoulders slumped slightly.

"Sorry," she murmured. "Sometimes I just get…irritated."

There's a freakin' understatement, Elizabeth thought, and had to bite her lip to keep from letting out a cackle of near-hysterical laughter. In the semi-shadows of the dark church basement, where they were sleeping on cots with about fifty other women, Liz's face was shadowed and her dark nature seemed perilously close to the surface.

How long since she's killed?

There'd been the two men when they'd escaped the first time from the gymnasium, but that had been so quick and so clearly in self-defense and unplanned that Elizabeth did not put it into the same category as Liz's other…extracurricular activities.

She leaned closer, close enough for Liz to feel her breath against her cheek, warm and smelling slightly of peppermint from the small tube of toothpaste they'd been given when they'd checked in that evening after five o'clock.

She sucked in a breath and asked in a whisper what she really wanted to know. "How many people have you actually killed?"

Liz twisted a little, placing a hand on Elizabeth's shoulder and leaning forward as if she might finally kiss her, but she was only aiming for her ear. Elizabeth was almost certain she felt Liz's lips brush her ear. Liz smelled of chewing gum; she'd found or stolen a pack somewhere. "Lots," she breathed, so low that only Elizabeth could hear her just barely. "Lots and lots."

Elizabeth shivered. Liz removed her hand from Elizabeth's shoulder and sat back. Elizabeth leaned back so her head was no longer close to Liz. She studied Liz and thought the girl looked very pleased with herself; a faint smug smile played about her lips, and in her eyes was triumph and something else. Something that looked like, could it be…yes…nostalgia.

Elizabeth continued to shiver, suddenly feeling very cold, and for no reason she remembered her dream from way back when she'd been sleeping curled next to a snake, a deadly snake that could shed its skin like a veil, but that would never change what it was.

Liz smiled at her, a smile of knowing and no warmth. "Good night, Elizabeth," she said, her voice oddly formal and with a strange, almost old-world syntax and accent as if English were not quite her first language. It was just one of the many things that was alien about her, and Liz was so *very* alien.

She watched as Liz crawled under her blanket, drew her legs up slightly, shoved one arm under her pillow and curled up to sleep, seeming as untroubled as a baby.

Elizabeth *was* troubled. She was troubled all that long and dark night, and there was no sleep for her but that which came in dreams, and the dreams were perhaps even worse than the waking nightmare or at least a continuation of it. For certainly sleep brought no respite.

Summer in New York, and she was asleep in her bed. The window was open because her apartment had no air-conditioning, and anyway she was on the second floor so who could get in? Now she was writing a paper and maybe this could be called How I Spent My Summer Vacation or Why I Hate New York, but it all boiled down to the same hot summer night, summer in the city, and she hated it with a passion.

Sleeping soundly, and suddenly there were people in the bed with her, and surely she was still dreaming, so she struggled awake. The military and her decision to join was less than a year away now, and this would have something to do with it, wouldn't it, something to do with a deep down desire to kill that wouldn't go away because she'd been tricked, they'd gotten the best of her all right, and all the tough talk in the world wouldn't change what happened in the dark that night. It didn't change the fact that the two had stuffed her own underwear in her mouth to keep her from screaming, that they'd taken turns, first raping her, then shoving her legs over her head and sticking it in her ass at which point she'd tried to scream, but had almost choked on her underwear, and the only thought that kept recurring, that made her vomit a little in her mouth, was that the underwear wasn't even that clean, she hadn't changed it for a couple of days, and that was not the worst indignity, but it seemed to be the final one, if that made any sense. They'd also taken turns punching her, calling her a fucking bitch while tears streamed silently down her face because she didn't even know these men, had never seen either of them in her life, but they hated her guts for no reason other than the fact that she had a cunt and so this is what she was good for. It seemed to go on forever, and maybe in some way, it still was going on. But finally they'd pounded her into unconsciousness, not with their cocks but their fists, and when she'd woken up, it was still dark out and only the pain in her body and the blood and jizz drying on her legs told her this hadn't been a dream.

Still crying, she'd gone into the bathroom, avoiding the mirror, and crawled into the bath, not scalding hot water: no matter what the goddamn books told you, she wasn't in the mood for any more pain, and even lukewarm water made the rips in her anus smart, and the water filled with a light red, so she drained and rinsed again and again, still crying. Then she limped back to the bedroom and tore off the sheets and threw them in the corner on the floor and collapsed back onto the mattress where she passed out for several more hours and when she woke up, it was daylight, and Saturday, so she didn't have to work, but inside of her it was still dark, and filling her was not just the shame and sadness, but a deep dark fissure full of rage that was growing and cracking...

"Elizabeth?" a voice whispered, and she swam gratefully out of sleep, relieved to be away from a darkness that brought no peace or rest. The voice belonged to Liz. She was propped up on her cot on her elbow, head resting on her hand, looking at Elizabeth. The darkness in her eyes from earlier was gone, and maybe Elizabeth had only imagined the depth of that darkness (but no, not really; even now she knew better than that) but whatever darkness had been there earlier was gone. Now those dark eyes were perfectly wide open and showing only concern.

"What?" Elizabeth whispered back.

"Are you okay?"

"Yeah. Why?"

"Because you're crying."

Elizabeth touched her cheek. It was true. Her cheeks were wet. She felt a scream rise up in her throat and quickly swallowed it back; all the words she would have spoken over the years swallowed back down, waiting, ready to emerge someday in a scream that would shake the world to its core, and wouldn't it deserve it, how could it not, how could it continue to spin after shattering her as it had done? And maybe that day would come still, the day she would scream, but it was not here, not tonight, so she just shoved her fist in her mouth and bit down hard then stared at Liz with blank eyes.

"I'm fine," she said, and rolled over, showing Liz her back, pretending to sleep as if she could do such a thing. For she never spoke of the rape, never even called it a rape in her mind, it was always "assault" as if she'd been mugged in a subway station. The idea of therapy or police was enough to want to make her scream with laughter because she, who was so horrible with faces due to a head injury when she was seven, knew damn well she'd never recognize the men who'd done it to her, even in a lineup, assuming they could ever catch them, and as for therapy, the idea only made her furious: some asshole pretending to understand. Unless they'd ever lain with blood drying on their thighs, Elizabeth wasn't interested in hearing a goddamn thing they had to say, and if they ever *had* lain in such a position then they *knew* there wasn't anything that could be said. Some things are simply done (but never truly over, are they?) when they are done, and words can later try and make of it something it never was, try and give meaning and form to that which has none, but the truth is always in the pain and the dark.

I think I know how Liz can kill.

And that dark part of Elizabeth's mind where sun never shone slowly turned on its axis, creaking, thinking, and she imagined joining Liz, somehow hunting down the men who'd done this to her for wouldn't Liz understand? Yes. They'd never discussed it in so many words, but Elizabeth was willing to bet her life that Liz had experience, firsthand experience, in an "assault" of the sort that Elizabeth had endured.

What might we do?

She imagined them flying through the night on a motorcycle, the arms of one around the waist of the other, entwined, hair blowing behind them, laughing, teeth red and stained with blood, wild animals that have finally fought back and the night would buckle and yield before them, bowing away in deference for they would own the night, and the image was sweet and good.

She rolled back over, facing Liz. If Liz was awake, she would get up and join her in the cot, snuggle next to her, wrap her arms around her and damn the consequences, and what it might mean. Tonight, she did not fear the darkness in Liz; tonight she understood it perfectly and was willing to take that step forward to embrace it, both literally and figuratively.

But Liz had gone back to sleep. Elizabeth sighed inwardly, but there was nothing to do but wait for the night to pass.

Daylight was a long time coming.

* * *

The next morning, after being served their hot breakfast in the church, the women were turned out onto the street. It was a shelter rule. Everyone out by eight a.m. and no one in before five p.m. They wandered the streets aimlessly, hands in pockets. At least Liz wandered aimlessly. Elizabeth seemed more like a pacing animal, her jaw clenched, shadows under her eyes and thinking deeply—brooding—on something. Liz glanced at her from time to time, but let her be. Elizabeth would talk when she was good and ready, and if she didn't want to talk, nothing would make her.

By eleven a.m., Liz had nearly given up on Elizabeth talking, and was considering ditching her to see if she could find somewhere to bum some smokes when Elizabeth finally broke her silence.

"We need to practice our powers and find out what we can do together," she said, as if they'd been talking all morning and this was merely a continuation of the discussion.

"What?" Liz asked in confusion.

"Practice our powers," Elizabeth said, looking at her intently. "Everything changed—for both of us—when you came into the picture. And now that you're here, there's a great many things we can do together that we couldn't before."

Liz smiled, a rich, dark smile, as images of fire and dark and chaos rose up. Yes. She would make them all pay. There would be burning and retribution, and at the end of it all, a great fire to cleanse everything. She imagined herself running across America, never tiring, a great blazing trail of fire behind her. How lovely...to set it all to burn.

"What did you have in mind?" she asked.

"Retribution," Elizabeth said tersely, and Liz's heart soared, for finally they were on the same page, sharing the same dream.

"Yes," she said emphatically.

"The Subset," Elizabeth continued. "We find them. We shut them down. Otherwise they win. They'll always have us on the run, fearing them. Maybe...just maybe...it's time they feared us." She turned to Liz, smiling grimly, not noticing how Liz's own smile faded then fell slowly to the pavement, withered and died.

The Subset. Of course. Elizabeth wanted to bring down the Subset. Liz, though...Liz did not care so much about the

Subset. To her, they were just another in a long line of people who did what they wanted to because they could. And most of the time, they got away with it. But sometimes you made your own justice and that's what she was all about. Making justice. Setting the score right. In her blood, she knew she was on her own. She did not think the Subset was so bad. She'd seen and experienced worse things than being imprisoned in a gym and taking a thumping. She'd rather go after more violent and vicious predators than some nebulous government agency especially as she did not think she and Elizabeth really could take down the Subset. In all likelihood, it was like the Hydra's head. Cut off one, and more would grow to take its place. Sure, they could kill some of the Subset. Thin the ranks. But undoubtedly there were hundreds more people in the wings, waiting to take over. No. The best way was to fight one by one against the worst of the worst of the offenders. You could never take them all out, but that was okay because the idea wasn't to create a perfect world. The idea was simply to make the world just a little bit better by taking out a scumbag who otherwise would have brought only pain and horror.

"You're fighting a useless battle," she said to Elizabeth.

Elizabeth stopped and faced her on the sidewalk. They'd reached a bus stop where there was a bench. Liz, who was tired, took the opportunity to sit down and rest. Elizabeth remained standing.

"You won't help me?" she said quietly, almost threatening, and Liz didn't care for that tone at all, but she didn't let it bother her. She had another plan forming in her mind.

"I didn't say that."

"Then you *will* help me?"

"Yes…"

Elizabeth's face lit up with surprise and happiness.

"If you help me," Liz continued, and a wary look came over Elizabeth's face.

"Help you what?" she asked.

"You know damned well," Liz said. "You know what I am, and you have for a long time. So quit jerking my dick and playing stupid."

"Are you asking for help in killing people?" Elizabeth asked quietly, finally sitting on the bench next to Liz and glancing quickly up and down the sidewalk to make sure no one was within earshot. The morning and the street were quiet and the buildings rundown and the people in them knew all too well how to mind their own business.

"Not people," Liz explained patiently. "Scumbags. Child rapists. Pedophiles. Animals that make your Subset look like kids playing Spy Versus Spy."

Elizabeth stared at the toes of the battered white sneakers she'd been given at the church, and the frayed cuffs of jeans that were slightly too large. She looked down on her luck, she had not a penny to her name, but she was surviving, and mentally, she felt stronger than she had in years. And hadn't she known from the moment she and Liz were thrown together that inevitably it would come to this? They would have to discuss what Liz was, and Elizabeth would have to decide how she felt about that. She'd taken the high road early on because…well, perhaps because she knew how easy it would have been to take the low road, to approve of it because some part of her *did* approve of what Liz did. Just not the pleasure Liz took in it.

Elizabeth had never liked compromises, but each of them had an agenda, and that agenda required the cooperation of the other to succeed on a grand scale. Otherwise they could go their separate ways, and Liz would continue her killing on a small scale until inevitably she was caught and ended her days in prison or taking the needle. And Elizabeth would spend the rest of her life living under false names in shelters, owning her freedom but nothing else. Once freedom had seemed like enough. Now she wanted more. She wanted to call the shots. She wanted a real life, a full one, a rich one. Something close to normal. And like it or not, Liz would have to be a part of making that happen.

"What do you have in mind?" she asked finally, looking up.

A smile slowly spread across Liz's face. She leaned over on the bench and began whispering in Elizabeth's ear. And the rest, really, was easy.

* * *

Liz and Elizabeth moved into a room together in a women's shelter that made arrangements for more permanent housing than the overnight shelters for the indigent in which they'd previously been taking refuge. It was in here that Liz suggested cutting Elizabeth's hair. Elizabeth, who'd been growing out her mane for years, touched it protectively.

"But why?" she asked.

"Because if anyone is looking for us, your hair is a main point of description. Cut it, and if we both dye our hair, we can maybe throw them off the trail a little."

Elizabeth shrugged. She didn't really want to cut her hair, but she wasn't appalled by the idea either and what Liz said did make a great deal of sense.

"Fine," she said wearily. "Cut it."

Liz was able to borrow some scissors. She came back smiling and flicking the scissors in the air.

"Let's do this shit," she said gleefully.

"You needn't look so delighted," Elizabeth commented, settling cross-legged on her bed.

Liz sat behind her and ran her fingers lightly through Elizabeth's hair, smoothing it. Her fingers felt nice. Maybe that was the real reason she didn't want her hair cut; people seldom touched it but on the rare occasions when they did, it felt very soothing.

Liz picked up Elizabeth's brush from the night table and combed the hair. She was surprisingly gentle. "You have gorgeous hair," she said. "I've always wanted straight hair."

Elizabeth laughed. "Nuts. I always wanted a natural wave like you have."

Liz giggled and they sat in a pleasant camaraderie, Liz stroking Elizabeth's hair for several long minutes.

Finally she picked up the scissors, snipped the air once and then, holding Elizabeth's hair carefully and tenderly, she began cutting. Elizabeth felt oddly exhilarated with every long lock that came off. No more hair weighing her down. Her head felt very light and free.

"All done," Liz said about twenty minutes later.

Elizabeth stood up and walked over to the full-length mirror on the back of the door. The haircut did not look bad nor did it make her face look round as she'd feared it might. On the contrary, it emphasized the high planes of her cheekbones and the strength of her individual features. Rather than a blunt cut, Liz had layered it so it was a shag cut rather similar to her own. Elizabeth touched it and smiled. Liz had come up and was standing behind her, just off to one side.

"Like it?" she asked with a hint of trepidation.

"Love it."

Liz smiled and reached out and brushed the hair back from Elizabeth's left ear. Elizabeth smiled and stepped away so that Liz wasn't quite so close to her. "What next?" she asked.

"We color it," Liz said.

"What color should we do?" Elizabeth asked.

"I'm bleaching mine and going red," Liz said. "As for you, I'd keep it simple and just go brunette. Maybe with the tips tinted blue. That'd look cool."

"Generational differences," Elizabeth said automatically, and Liz laughed, picked up her pillow and took a swipe at Elizabeth.

"You know you want to, you old fart," she said.

"Whippersnapper," Elizabeth said, biting back a laugh and smacking Liz with her own pillow. Giggling they began swatting each other with pillows, laughing, chasing each other, and then shrieking until someone pounded on the wall.

Both women went still. Liz pulled a face of mock surprise and raised one finger to her lips.

"Shhh," she whispered, imitating Elmer Fudd. "Be vewwy vewwy quiet. We hunting wabbit."

Elizabeth's face had turned beet red and her eyes filled with tears as she tried not to laugh aloud, clamping her hand over her own mouth. Liz began taking exaggerated, slow, quiet steps across the room, still carrying her pillow and pretending to be Elmer Fudd. Elizabeth let out one loud snort of laughter.

Liz giggled and began making soft snorting sounds as she got on all fours and pretended to be rooting around on the floor. "You sound like you're rooting for truffles," she whispered. She snorted a couple of times and rooted some more. Elizabeth curled up on her bed, shaking, tears streaming down her face as she held back her laughter.

Liz sat on the floor. Elizabeth in hysterics made her giggle too, both women muffling the giggles so they wouldn't disturb their neighbors.

* * *

Four days later, two women were working in the kitchen of the Mercy Shelter for Women. One was a tiny petite redhead, the other a handsome solid-looking brunette. Both had short shaggy hair and what stood out was not their looks (both were cute, but neither would turn heads on the street) but the extraordinary synchronicity they seemed to possess. They seldom spoke more than a word or two to one another, but when one needed something, the other knew it and was there with it. Outsiders, other women working in the kitchen, sensed the invisible circle around these two and wondered privately if they were lovers. The wiser ones sensed a bond deeper than love, one which spoke of understanding, and that was even more rare than love.

They were right on this count. Elizabeth and Liz had begun sleeping together though it was still strictly platonic. They'd bought a nightlight for the room to help with Liz's fear of the dark, a silly nightlight with a black cat on it which Liz liked very much, but she still had frequent nightmares, and Elizabeth found out another interesting thing about her as well: she sleepwalked. Not every night, not even most nights, but it happened. The first was about two weeks after they'd begun sharing a room. Elizabeth woke up to see that Liz had gotten out of bed and was standing in the center of the room, very rigid, eyes wide open. The curtains were cracked a little, revealing the streetlight which cast a faint yellow pallor over the white walls.

"Liz?" Elizabeth murmured, still half asleep, pushing herself up to see her better.

"I wouldn't do that," Liz said clearly in a monotone. "She's still very depressed."

"What?"

There was no answer. Elizabeth sat up on the edge of the bed, wearing her new blue men's pajamas that she'd finally been able to afford with the pocket money they earned by working in the kitchen. She looked at Liz who was staring straight ahead with a frozen expression, then got up and took Liz's arm.

"Liz?"

Liz stared ahead, her eyes not tracking Elizabeth at all. Elizabeth shook her arm. "Liz!" she said sharply, her voice louder.

"Huh?" Liz blinked. She stared at Elizabeth's hand on her arm, then looked around, her eyes growing wild. "What's going on?"

"You were sleepwalking."

Astonishingly, Liz looked about to cry.

"I don't sleepwalk!" she yelled and ran to her bed, throwing herself facedown on it. Someone next door pounded on the wall. Liz sat up, her face furious and looking tear-streaked, though maybe it was only the light, and pounded right back. Elizabeth hurried over and sat on the edge of the bed. Liz had buried her face in the pillow and was breathing hard. Was she crying? Uncertainly, Elizabeth patted her back gently. Liz responded like a love-starved animal, turning and burrowing her face in Elizabeth's lap. She reminded Elizabeth of the first night they'd met when Liz had also been frightened. She stroked Liz's hair.

"Sleepwalking is not a big deal," she said gently. "A lot of people do it now and then."

Liz mumbled something.

"What?"

Liz lifted her head. Her face was tear-streaked. Elizabeth could only chalk it up to exhaustion or perhaps just one of Liz's inexplicable mood swings.

"I don't want to be any more a freak than I already am," Liz said, her voice unhappy.

"You're not a freak," Elizabeth said, though she didn't really believe it.

Liz apparently didn't either because she smiled a little and took hold of Elizabeth's hand. "You're nice to say that," she said. "But I think maybe you're not being entirely honest. Still—I appreciate that you care enough about my feelings to lie." She smiled tremulously.

Elizabeth laughed, not really sure why. Liz was just funny sometimes, especially when she wasn't trying to be funny. Still holding Liz's hand, she stroked Liz's soft wavy hair. "Are you better now?" she asked.

Liz suddenly looked panicked. "Don't leave me!" she begged. "Please. We don't have to do anything, I just…I don't want to sleep alone."

She stared, and even in the dark Elizabeth could see the pleading and the need in those big brown eyes. She sent a doubtful glance at the bed; it was a twin, as were all the beds in the women's shelter—no hanky-panky would be going on under the suspicious eyes of the Sisters of Mercy—then pulled back the sheet and climbed in, snuggling next to Liz and wrapping her arms around her. Liz burrowed in next to her, and Elizabeth could faintly smell her hair which she'd washed just before bed. Coconut shampoo that made her hair very soft. Elizabeth smiled, struck by the sudden desire to kiss the top of Liz's head, but afraid it would be taken the wrong way. Still feeling self-conscious, she simply held her.

They slept that way, and for the next couple of weeks, the routine was much the same. They did their chores in the day, and at night snuggled together like two children in the dark. Elizabeth didn't say it aloud and neither did Liz, but all day they looked forward to nightfall when they could go to bed. With the lights off, the room became a haven, a warm burrow where they could nestle together in their tiny patch of safety, the bed like an island where no harm could come to them if they were together. Sometimes Elizabeth thought about the gun that she used to sleep with in New Mexico, and how funny it was that when she was with Liz, she didn't miss it, didn't feel the need of it.

Liz was warm and soft and she smelled good. She didn't kick, she didn't snore, and her way of sleeping was cute because regardless of her dark side, she often wore a faint smile as she slept, as if her dreams were of a better world than this one. Or maybe it was just that the presence of Elizabeth made her feel safe, just as Elizabeth's own nightmares seemed to cease when she was holding Liz.

They also practiced their gift. Neither of them had ever been able to move objects on her own before solely by using her mind, but when they were together—they took turns levitating the cheap blond wood dresser and making it do the Funky Chicken from side to side.

Liz also pursued her extracurricular activities. Of this, Elizabeth wanted no part but she was aware of Liz's abrupt daytime disappearances after the morning work was done, often not returning until nightfall. Liz no longer invited Elizabeth to come out with her and that was just as well because Elizabeth would not have gone. Ostensibly Liz was looking for a job, but they both knew better; Liz had never done an honest day's work in her life, and she wasn't about to start now. No. Liz was hunting. Scouting out the next target. She'd visited the library and used the free Internet there to scour the local sex offender registry, looking for the most offensive people—and she used the term "people" lightly—that she could find. Repeat offenders, offenses involving children under the age of ten…there was no shortage of rotten fruit that needed to be pruned. After she settled on one, she went to where he lived and observed the area all day, trying to get an idea of his comings and goings. Her hunting routine never varied. That was a pattern that might one day lead her into trouble, and she knew it but it had worked just fine for the past five years, and she was loathe to change something that was working so well.

And this time…this time the kill would be very easy so long as Elizabeth cooperated. And Elizabeth would. Once Liz filled her in on all the details of what this man had done, Elizabeth would help. Elizabeth had never revealed any of her deep dark secrets aloud to Liz, but she didn't need to. Liz had wandered through the periphery of her dreams just often enough to see all that she needed to know, and even if she hadn't, she simply knew. She recognized other survivors, even the ones who had no powers, and she was drawn to them like a moth to flame because they *knew* and surely...surely, deep in their hearts, a small but perfect flame of hatred burned, just as it did inside Liz. Only she'd fanned hers into a blazing bonfire, and it made her strong.

To fight back was to be alive.

* * *

Byron Todd was smart, talented, good-looking. He had every material possession that most people wanted and none of them touched him because he didn't care about those things. What he cared about was power. Power over other people. He liked to know what made them tick, and usually figuring that out was easy because people were predictable: they wanted money or fame or women or love or families. Line up a million and ask them what their dreams were, and you would likely get five variations of the same theme. Thus most people bored him, and he viewed them as expendable. Elizabeth had intrigued him, not just because she had undefined psychic abilities but because she seemed to want nothing. He did not care for women in a sexual way or men either (such things bored him), but watching Elizabeth sitting in that little waiting room, perfectly passive and unmoving, he'd been riveted. Her friend, shrieking and pounding on the door, asking useless questions...now that he was used to. He'd seen that and expected it. He did not expect someone in a helpless situation to react...logically. And what Elizabeth had done was purely logical. She'd assessed the situation, seen no way out and so had calmly waited to see what would happen next. It was the *only* logical course of action. And yet of the hundred, the thousands, of people he'd observed in that little room, not one—not a single one—had ever reacted that way except her.

And then she'd dug the device out of her arm. It had taken them only three hours to realize what had happened, but that three hours had been enough to allow the women to elude them. To do such a thing took guts, and he'd seen plenty of guts in his line of work, and he always admired it. Elizabeth had taken root in the back of his mind like a loose tooth; you knew the best thing was to leave it be and let it come out in its own good time, but your tongue couldn't resist wiggling it, pushing at it. Elizabeth and Liz were like that to him. What were they to each other? Something about the two of them nagged at the back of his mind, a strangeness in their relationship and yet... some sort of pattern.

Then something occurred to him. Something so fundamentally obvious that he was sure it *must* have already been done, but still... He wanted to see for himself. Because if there was even a possibility of what he was thinking...It did not seem possible, but he dismissed that thought because he'd seen enough to know that everything was possible. Everything and then some. He got up from his bed.

He wore black silk pajamas and slept alone. His apartment was furnished in classic modern with lots of black leather, chrome, and hardwood floors. A maid came twice weekly. He went over to the closet where there were numerous Gucci gray suits hanging there, all tailored to fit him perfectly. He quickly showered and dressed, grabbed the keys to his Porsche, set the alarm system and left, heading just down the road to the Compound. It was an hour's drive and it was four a.m., the back road deserted, but the drive seemed to take no time at all. He removed his ID badge from the glove box and entered with no problem—he had top clearance.

In the lab, always one to observe proper protocol, he donned a white coat, and then he opened the refrigerator and found the vials marked with Elizabeth's and Liz's ID numbers. He removed the vials and checked the paperwork to see the tests that had been performed. Incredible. There'd been a handful of tests, but not the one he was looking for. Initially there'd been several vials of blood from each as the tests required so much per sample, but this...this would barely take any time at all.

He set up. Tested. And there it was.

He stepped back, a slow bewildered smile spreading over his face. He was so seldom taken by surprise, it was a delight when it happened, better than any orgasm. He checked again just to be sure. Yes.

The DNA had been tested separately for all kinds of elements but never compared. He'd run a simple comparison and found the most shocking and yet easy aspect to have been overlooked.

The DNA for the two women was identical.

CHAPTER EIGHT

The man's name was Ted Scranton. Liz whispered in Elizabeth's ear the details of everything he'd done to little girls, embellishing what she didn't know for sure, whispering on and on even after Elizabeth pulled away, covered her ears and begged her to stop. Liz would not stop; it was real, it was here, and it needed to be dealt with. She had followed him for just over a month. Now she was ready to take him out in a way that she'd never done before.

Now she and Elizabeth were crouched in the bushes outside his house, under the bedroom window. They'd taken the city bus to a stop about a mile away and then walked the rest of the way. It was seven p.m. and the sun had just set. The cicadas were singing, and the night was balmy and dark.

Normally Liz would have had her Bowie knife with her, but tonight there should be no need of a Bowie knife. With Elizabeth beside her, she could do everything that needed doing. It would be an interesting experiment.

The house was an ordinary split-level Florida home. There was a lanai in the back though no pool, and Scranton lived alone, something that would make the job much easier.

From where they were crouched, they heard the sound of the garage door opening and closing. A car door slamming. Waiting and waiting. Then the bedroom light flicked on. Liz could wait no longer. She stood up, peering through the window. Scranton stood at his dresser, putting his watch and wallet on it. He was a tall man with black hair in an almost military-style cut and with a bit of a beer belly. She imagined what she'd do if she was physically big enough…and then she did it with her mind. She threw him on the bed. She ripped at his clothes.

"*What the hell?!*" Liz and Elizabeth could hear him yelling even through the window. Liz shoved one of his socks in his mouth. Abruptly, Elizabeth, who had stood up to watch, turned around and crouched on the ground, dry-heaving. Liz ignored her; she did not need Elizabeth's participation, only her presence from which to feed. She imagined his skin being peeled from his body slowly and watched as it happened.

I can do anything. No one can stop me.

She made one eye explode. She twisted his nose then broke it. He was no longer moving, having passed out when his skin was halfway peeled from his body, but he was still breathing. Liz thought about shoving the leg of a chair up his ass, but suddenly she no longer wanted to be here. She snapped his neck roughly to the side.

"He's dead," she announced calmly, turning to look at Elizabeth who was crouched on the grass on all fours, her skin looking very pale and clammy in the dim light. "Let's go." She held out a hand.

Elizabeth shied away. "Don't touch me!"

Liz rolled her eyes. "Whatever." She paused. "Do you wanna get ice cream on the way back? I'm craving Ben and Jerry's for some reason."

Elizabeth stood up. Her legs were shaking. She stared at Liz as if she'd just started giving birth to a litter of two-headed kittens. "I—no. No ice cream. Just home."

Liz shrugged. "Okay."

They crept along through backyards, ducking out of sight when they spotted lights on, and in this stealthy way made their way out of the neighborhood and back to the bus stop. Under the light at the bus stop, Liz had a better view of Elizabeth and could see that she was very pale, almost ashen.

"Are you all right?" she asked solicitously.

Elizabeth just gave her that strange look again as if she'd never seen Liz before.

"You fucking tortured him!" she hissed finally.

Liz was surprised. "That's why you're upset? Good grief, I told you all those things he did to the little girls he caught. How he'd trick them into taking—"

"I don't care!" Elizabeth snapped, almost yelling. "He's a monster, so kill him, fine, I don't care about that either, not really, but when you take just as much pleasure in doing what you do as he does then how are you so different than him?"

Liz looked a little surprised by the outburst but not at all fazed. "Because I don't hurt children or innocents," she said calmly as if that made all the difference.

And some part of Elizabeth's mind had to admit…it did.

* * *

"How? How can their DNA be the same?" John Peters thundered. "Elizabeth has no twin." The mole by his nose was quivering wildly. He had been in charge of overseeing Elizabeth's training since day one and the idea that he might have overlooked an element this crucial was infuriating. Especially to know an ass like Byron Todd had discovered it, and then to have the news delivered by this young arrogant Opie lookalike in front of him.

The young Opie lookalike, who was actually thirty-seven and named Paul, had been on board long enough to know Peters and wasn't fazed in the slightest. "It's easy. She created Liz with her mind after she was…assaulted. It's what had been bothering me about those two. In some ways, they're identical but in others they're polar opposite. It was almost too neat. One quiet, one loud. One feisty, one phlegmatic. One impulsive, one rational. Elizabeth had two things going for her: her psychic ability and the vividness of her imagination. That woman can sit like a lump in a chair for twelve hours and never get bored as long as she has her mind and can daydream. After her assault, I think she really wanted revenge and simply put, she couldn't get it. She didn't know what her assailants looked like, she didn't know how to begin. All that rage went somewhere, and Liz was born, a shadow self, set free in the world. You've heard of multiple personality? Elizabeth is one but because of her abilities, her personality isn't just in her mind; it physically manifests as a real human being with will and influence in the world. It also explains Elizabeth's lethargy and incompleteness. It takes a lot of energy to live two lives. She has half the traits she needs to be a complete human being, and Liz has the other half."

Peters seemed to mull this over. His mole stopped quivering, and he sat down in the swivel chair behind his desk, some of the red flush draining from his face. "So what do we do?"

"Integrate them," Paul said in that matter-of-fact tone. He remained standing. "She has that much power which is why it doesn't work unless they're together, but split like this, they're too irrational to work with."

"Huh." Peters chewed on his lip for a moment, a rare moment of doubt for his own abilities creeping in. "Can we find them?"

"Of course. Just scour the papers for unsolved murders of sexual offenders. Our Liz is about due for a strike." Paul smiled at this last part. He'd majored in criminology in college, and he'd been quite good at it.

"It'll take a few days to start working our way out from here," Peters warned. "And if she's left the country, it will be very difficult."

"We'll cross that bridge when we come to it," Paul said, knowing that there was no way Liz or Elizabeth could have obtained false passports that would hold up under any kind of scrutiny, not on their own with no known resources or friends to help, but he was also savvy enough to know that Peters just needed to get the last word.

"Then proceed," Peters ordered curtly, folding his stubby fingers together decisively atop his desk.

"Yes, sir." Paul gave an almost over-the-top obsequious little bow and exited silently, almost slithering like a deadly snake, Peters thought.

He did not trust that man. But Paul was good at what he did, and in the Subset, results trumped the ability to seem human or even likable.

* * *

There was no snuggling between Liz and Elizabeth back at the shelter the night of the murder. Elizabeth had no desire to be physically near Liz. Every time she looked at Liz, she remembered standing up in the grass, peeking briefly through the window, and seeing that man with his skin halfway off, sinew and muscle exposed but, worst of all, still alive, eyeballs rolling wildly in their sockets, trying to scream and unable to because of the fucking sock. Though it hadn't been underwear in his mouth—at least that was something. She'd fallen back to her knees, and she'd sensed when he'd finally lost consciousness from terror and pain, but it had taken a long time—a very long time. And she knew damn well Liz was aware of it too. The difference was that Liz simply didn't care. She'd been smug and enjoying the power she had over Scranton.

How much empathy has to be lost to reach that point?

Elizabeth didn't know but she suspected it was a lot.

As for Liz…she was tired of Elizabeth's dramatics. Elizabeth had known full well what she was getting into when she went to Scranton's house. For God's sake, the woman was a bounty hunter; she tracked down serial killers who often tortured their victims. Yet all of a sudden she was acting like a housewife who'd never even thought of reality until she saw it. Fucking hypocrite. It pissed Liz off, because on some level, she was sure that Elizabeth had known exactly what she was going to do, had tacitly approved of it…and then, seeing the reality, finked out.

At breakfast, Elizabeth stayed in bed while Liz went downstairs and ate a hearty meal of an omelet and ham. After breakfast, they should have gone to work in the kitchen, cleaning up and preparing lunch for the house but Elizabeth begged off, crying sick. Liz smiled sweetly and covered for her, seething inside.

"You fucking hypocrite," she hissed. After lunch when she was finally able to get back to their room, Elizabeth, in her pajamas, was still in bed.

"Leave me alone, Liz," she said wearily.

Liz had no intention of leaving her alone. "No. You knew damn well what I am, and you agreed to it, and now you're acting shocked and treating me like I'm some sort of monster. Don't play stupid. You knew from the beginning what the score was so why the dramatics now?"

"I'm not denying anything," Elizabeth said. "Okay? I take full responsibility for my part in this. It's just—there's a world of difference between 'knowing' something and actually *seeing* it done before your very eyes."

Liz was quiet for a few moments, thinking this over. "Fair enough," she admitted. "And whatever, you held up your end of the bargain so when you're ready…I'll help you. Deal?"

"I don't know," Elizabeth said. "My plan may have changed."

"Changed how?"

"To bring down the Subset, we have to go back and face them. Which would mean letting them capture us again."

"Oh fuck that! You're insane if you think I'll agree to that. I'm not going back there."

"I didn't ask you to. I'm just thinking aloud, that's all. You do realize they'll be coming for us soon enough now, don't you?"

"What?" Liz sat down on her bed. "Why?"

"Because of what you did. A crime like that…in a suburban Florida neighborhood against a white man with money? It makes news."

"Why would they connect it with me?" Liz asked quickly.

"Because *I* know what you are. Ergo…*they* know what you are. They've had people on staff who can read my mind for years. I'm sure they know more about my past and all my secrets than I do."

"I didn't see any people like that," Liz said uneasily.

Elizabeth just shrugged. "Why *would* you see them? I doubt they could read minds from three states over, but from the next room? That's nothing."

"Do you think…do you think they read my mind?" Liz asked warily.

Her mind was very compartmentalized. There were experiences she'd made her peace with, but only on the assumption that no one ever knew about them. It made them all less real. Now Elizabeth was telling her calmly that all her secrets were nothing, that someone had rummaged through her mind and knew even her deepest and darkest of secrets. And she did it so damn calmly!

Elizabeth just shrugged. Was a tiny part of her enjoying Liz's discomfort? Yes…she thought it might be. And she felt no apologies for that. "I can't see why they wouldn't," she said.

Liz's hands curled into tight little fists. "Fuckers," she muttered.

"It's a tough old world," Elizabeth muttered.

Liz gave her a dirty look. "You needn't act so smug. Your hands are as dirty as mine."

"I never said they weren't." Elizabeth got up. She didn't want to be with Liz anymore. "I'm going downstairs to help with dinner."

On the way past the dresser, she bent down and removed the nightlight from the wall, then tossed it in the trash with a cool look at Liz. "You don't need that. You don't have to be afraid of the dark. Hell, the dark should be afraid of you."

She left. Liz glared after her, raging inside.

Acting like she's better than me. As if butter wouldn't melt in her mouth. Bitch.

Liz hated being looked down upon, and through so much of her life she had been. But there was more to it than that, wasn't there? Yes. If she was honest, it was the murder of Ted Scranton that pointed to it. He was a repeat child rapist, a pedophile who'd deserved exactly what he got, and no matter what Elizabeth on her holier-than-thou trip might say, Liz was sure the parents of the little girls that had been raped were losing no sleep anymore because of Ted Scranton. But nonetheless...the kill bothered her. It bothered her because it had not been satisfying. There'd been no intimacy. In the past, even in the slash-and-run kills, there'd been that one second at least where the killer had looked into her eyes, and they'd recognized each other completely. It was the only connection Liz ever felt. Until Elizabeth. The first friend she'd ever had. Who was now acting as if Liz were some sort of piece of trash.

Fuck her.

She got up, threw her small stash of clothes into a backpack she'd been given from Goodwill. She didn't need Elizabeth. She didn't need anyone. She stopped by the trash and looked in at her nightlight, debating fishing it out. Screw it, she decided. Elizabeth was right; she didn't need to fear the dark. Let the dark fear her.

* * *

One week later, Liz had stolen a car and was sleeping rough in an RV park in Jacksonville, Florida. Sometimes she had crazy thoughts. Dreams. Nightmares. About killing. Not the animals she'd disposed of so far, they didn't count, but about shooting high-profile people, corrupt politicians. The blood ran red in her dreams, and when she woke up she sometimes felt it on her skin as if she'd been bathing in it and it was crusted under her nails. She always woke early, in full dark, and would wait with bated breath for the sun to rise and though she could feel the blood, she could never see it: she was still clean. Then, and only then, would she be able to breathe and move again.

She thought about Elizabeth often, but it just made a dull rage rise up inside of her. Elizabeth had betrayed her. Liz was not exactly sure of how that had happened, but in her mind, that was just the way it had gone down, and she'd become so convinced of this that it was now fully real to her and her rage grew every day. She thought if she ever saw Elizabeth again, she just might kill her.

She didn't think that she ever would see Elizabeth again.

* * *

Better off without her. Better off without her. Elizabeth told herself that over and over. She knew it was true. Liz was a mess and a monster, and she was better off without her. It didn't change the fact that she missed the smell of coconut shampoo in the night or the warmth of Liz's hand holding her own, Liz's body curled into hers. Sometimes she thought of their pillow fight or other times they'd laughed together. They'd laughed a great deal considering the grimness of their situation. Elizabeth slept a lot and did her chores, and when she wasn't working in the shelter, she curled up in forgotten corners and read. She was soft-spoken and never ever got mad or involved in the house drama. Sometimes other women commented on how "sweet" she was.

My temper has up and left me, Elizabeth thought wryly. And it was true in some way she couldn't define. She and Liz had completed each other. She told herself she was doing fine, and if life was sometimes empty and she didn't feel quite real or quite whole, wasn't that just part of getting older? Sure. Sure it was.

And then the doors were kicked in. Not literally. The Subset simply entered the house, and Elizabeth, who was curled up in the dayroom reading a worn copy of *Ramona and Beezus* (she found comfort in rereading her childhood favorites and did not consider it odd for a grown woman to frequently read chapter books meant for eight-year-olds) suddenly felt the matron of the house tap her on the shoulder.

"Miss Elizabeth? The police are here. They want to speak to you."

Her plain elongated face behind her spectacles looked worried. She was no stranger to police showing up at the shelter, but it never boded well for anyone involved.

It's Liz. Something to do with Liz, Elizabeth thought anxiously. She swallowed nervously and went into the kitchen. A young attractive man in his early thirties with dark hair, wearing a Florida state police uniform, was standing there.

"Elizabeth Highsmith?" he asked.

"Yes?"

"Could you step outside with me for a minute? I have some questions about a friend of yours, Liz Thompson."

Don't go, Elizabeth thought suddenly. It's a trap. She turned to run. Another "officer" was standing there, holding a hypodermic which he slipped into her neck. And then all went black.

* * *

Again, Elizabeth woke up in a small lead-lined room. This time she was asleep on a full-size bed wearing a gray sweatsuit. Liz was passed out next to her, also in matching clothes.

The room was about the size of her bedroom back in Albuquerque but considerably more sparse. The walls were a plain white with no decorations. She tried to raise her hand to brush a strand of hair from her face. Her hand rose about three inches then stopped, and she felt something cool and metal dig into her wrist. She looked down in surprise.

She was handcuffed to Liz. Marvelous. The slight tug of her wrist made Liz stir. She opened her eyes, blinked, winced, then looked over and saw Elizabeth. For a moment, her face lit up with delight. Then abruptly it became truculent and closed.

"You," she said.

"Yeah. And you."

They were both silent.

"I have to pee," Liz said finally.

Wonderful, Elizabeth thought. Nonetheless she stood up and together she and Liz made their way over to the toilet which this time was sitting in a corner of the room. The Subset was not big on providing privacy for toilets. With Elizabeth's help, Liz was able to do her business and then Elizabeth followed suit. After that, they looked briefly at each other then went and sat silently on the edge of the bed.

"You threw away my nightlight!" Liz burst out suddenly.

"You skinned a man alive," Elizabeth replied calmly, somehow feeling that should take precedence in the "awful things you have done" contest but not sure that it did. Liz seemed pretty upset about that nightlight.

"You know why I did what I did," Liz replied. "But I don't know why you did what you did."

Because you disturb me. You're like all the nasty little parts of myself that I'd want to throw away.

The thought came unbidden into her mind. Looking at Liz, that sweet young-looking face, the face of a girl next door, she felt that maybe it wasn't quite fair... There were aspects of Liz that she liked and even admired... But it was close to fair.

In the corner of the room there was the usual speaker and tiny camera, but nonetheless, both women jumped when a voice emanated from the speaker.

"Liz and Elizabeth?"

The women looked up in surprise. The voice was pleasant and well-modulated, ideal for being broadcast over speakers as if the man had been trained for just such a purpose, and who knows, Elizabeth thought, maybe he had. At any rate, when he had their full and undivided attention, he continued. "We'd like to send someone in to explain things to you. But we need your assurance that you won't hurt him."

Elizabeth had no desire to hurt anyone. She looked at Liz who appeared more perplexed than outraged at the comment. Liz nodded. "You have our word," Elizabeth said, addressing the loudspeaker once again.

"Very well."

A few minutes later, the door slid open and a tall man in his early thirties with a slightly crooked nose came in. He leaned against the wall, folding his arms, and looked at them with a smile that didn't reach his eyes, which were as smooth and empty as two brown marbles. "My name is Mr. Todd," he said. "I'm sure you both wonder why you're here today."

"You're very direct for a member of the Subset," Elizabeth countered, unsure what to make of this strange man. He was not what she was used to dealing with.

He shrugged modestly as if she'd paid him a compliment. "I believe there's a time for everything," he said, "and right now, the time for being direct with you—with both of you—is here. Do you know what I discovered recently?"

Elizabeth shook her head. She had no idea what he'd discovered but some prick of anxiety within told her that it probably wouldn't be good news.

"You two have identical DNA," he said, looking from one to the other and beaming as if this news should precipitate some kind of reaction.

It just left the two women bewildered. Mr. Todd saw that and sighed, shifting a little. "Do you know what that means?" he asked.

"We're...related?" Liz asked hesitantly.

Mr. Todd shook his head. "You wouldn't have identical DNA in that case. Normally only identical twins can have identical DNA."

"We're twins?" Elizabeth asked, her voice thick with disbelief.

Mr. Todd looked disgusted. "Do you think you look like twins?" he asked. "You're a little long in the tooth to be her twin, don't you think?"

Elizabeth didn't feel that last comment was entirely necessary, but she didn't take issue with it. This guy looked to be the type that was rude a lot of the time and probably wasn't even aware of it because he just didn't care. "So we're not twins," she said, with just a trace of irritation. "Then what is your point?"

"Think of any other way the two of you could have identical DNA," he said.

"We're clones," Liz offered.

"Close," Mr. Todd said, and his voice was just a little too smug for Elizabeth to hold back her irritation.

"So spit it out," she snapped. "Put up or shut up, as my momma would say." Her mother never would have said such a thing but it sounded pretty anyway, and it certainly fit the mood.

Mr. Todd looked a little irritated. "You," he said, pointing at Liz, "are the creation of her." He pointed at Elizabeth.

"What?"

Elizabeth wasn't sure who said the word. It could have been either of them or both of them. Or maybe nobody even needed to say it.

Mr. Todd unfolded his arms and stood up straight. For some reason, he reminded Elizabeth of a reptile, and she felt a shudder of fear.

"Your mind created Liz," he said. "Very similar to what happens in multiple personality disorder. A common—well, not common, but not unheard of—occurrence in the face of severe trauma. However, because of your abilities, Liz became a real person, containing aspects of your own personality that you rejected for whatever reason, and—" He broke off, alerted and then alarmed by the dark rage in Liz's face. Somehow, in all his fantasies of how this conversation might go, he'd never even conceived of the idea that he might get hurt.

Liz blew a hole in his chest.

"No!" Elizabeth screamed and grabbed at Liz's arm. It was rigid and wiry with taut muscle.

Out in the hall, they heard feet pounding. Neither woman moved. Elizabeth because she knew it was pointless, and Liz, because she did not care. Fuckers. Saying she wasn't real. She didn't know where that clown had been going with that crazy thought, but the whole idea of it bothered her enough that she'd…well, she'd done what she needed to do. Now she just felt sullen and ready to retreat within herself the way she did when dealing with cops. Elizabeth though…Elizabeth was staring at Mr. Todd and the neat little hole in his chest that had begun to spread and bloom into a small red flower. He was lying on the floor where'd he slipped down, back against the wall, legs splayed in front of him and the expression on his face was one of surprise.

"Why did you do that?" Elizabeth asked.

The footsteps had stopped outside the door, but no one came in.

"'Cause he deserve it," Liz said, her street slang accent especially thick and a little put-on, Elizabeth thought with irritation.

They'll fucking kill us, she thought miserably. But there was no killing to be done that night. The door slipped open. Six men in bulletproof vests, helmets and full SWAT team regalia were standing there with rifles. Two of them immediately trained the rifles on Liz and Elizabeth.

"One funny move outta either of you, and I blow you both to hell," he snapped.

Neither woman answered. Nor did they move. With military precision, the other four men retrieved the body of Mr. Todd and disappeared out the door. The two men with guns waited till they were safely out then followed and the door slid shut again.

Liz and Elizabeth looked at each other.

It's not possible, Elizabeth thought.

It is possible, she thought a moment later.

Liz was thinking much the same thing.

"I wonder…" she said. "How would we know if he was telling us the truth? Or if it was just bullshit?"

"What do you think it was?" Elizabeth asked carefully.

"I think it's—insane. Impossible. I'm not a goddamn figment of your imagination. I have a life. I remember my childhood. My parents. My mom is a heroin addict. I don't know who my dad was. I was in foster care from the time I was six until I was sixteen and ran away. You?"

"My mom was a lawyer. My dad was a dentist," Elizabeth said calmly. "They died when I was in freshman year of college."

Liz rolled her eyes. "Yeah, we're as alike as two peas in a fuckin' pod," she said. "If we were the same person, wouldn't we have the same frickin' memories?"

Elizabeth, who'd read a lot—an inordinate amount really—on the subject of Multiple Personality Disorder—MPD—knew better. "No," she said. "Generally, with MPD, each personality has its own background story. He never said we were the same person. He just said that I...created you." An image of Athena springing fully formed from the head of Zeus sprang to mind, and she smiled.

Liz looked incredulous. "You think this is funny?" she asked.

"Isn't everything?" Elizabeth countered back. After all, that was one of Liz's life philosophies. Everything was a joke. Not necessarily a *good* joke, but a joke.

Liz raised the manacled hand that was attached to Elizabeth's, grabbed Elizabeth's hand and bit it hard enough to draw blood.

Elizabeth screamed.

"That feel like a fuckin' figment to you?" Liz snapped.

Elizabeth pulled at the handcuff, trying to snap it loose with her mind, but Liz wasn't cooperating and resisted, and without the two of them working together, Elizabeth's powers were greatly diminished.

"He didn't say you were a figment," Elizabeth said, waving her hurt hand. "He said—ow, that hurts—damn you—that I created you. You're still real."

"I don't get it," Liz said sullenly.

"I don't either," Elizabeth admitted. "But suppose he's right? He basically claimed that we're—I—have multiple personalities, and you are or were one of my personalities. I wonder what they want from us?"

But deep down she knew. Everyone assumed there was only one good route for those with multiple personality.

Integration.

And she wondered who would get smothered and lost in

that process. Herself? Or Liz? But the answer, of course, was neither. If her reading on the subject was correct, neither of them was whole now—whatever that meant—and integration would mean a blurring of both them.

Annihilation.

CHAPTER NINE

In dreams that night, she knew why she and Liz had been chained together. The closer they were, the harder it was to keep the boundaries between them separate. She did not want to snuggle with Liz, and the tension writhed between them like a living thing, permeating the consciousness of them both. Elizabeth no longer wanted to snap the cuffs off Liz and free her. Disturbing as the presence of the other woman was in such close proximity, the idea of her running loose in the world was even more disturbing. On some deep level, her mind had begun to accept that she needed Liz to be whole.

Elizabeth didn't know about Liz, but for her sleep was a long time coming, and she was never entirely sure if she got to sleep or if her dreams simply merged with Liz's mind and her daydreams and memories became her nightmares and vice versa. Though really she only had one nightmare to share with Liz.

Maybe that was enough. Maybe it reflected itself, echoed throughout her mind, bouncing off the walls like light refracted against a thousand funhouse mirrors till the horror of it had tainted everything. It was possible. And Liz...Liz was made of cast-off nightmares, wearing them like a ragman who came in the night to feed off the forbidden fruits of a richer darker world where haints were common and nighttime was always eternal.

Liz's whole life was a nightmare. The mother who left her crying in her crib, wet with diaper rash and hungry for hours, while she was nodding out from drugs. Later, the older foster brother who liked to play doctor a little too much and too often with intense "examinations." Followed in adolescence by a new foster home and a foster father who took it further and simply fucked her when he felt the need till she finally ran away at sixteen. No, Liz had no good memories, or at best only a handful. Nothing to savor. She had been born of rage, and her memories, while not even real, were congruent with the personality that Elizabeth had left for her. Elizabeth, though hardly a child of light born to sing and dance, was still capable of being happy. There'd been sledding on cold days with her best friend and hot cocoa when she got home. The excitement of Halloween and all-night candy sharing with the same best friend. The comfort of long afternoons in the library curled up with her favorite chapter books. The fun of baseball season every year, and riding her bike in the fall. Elizabeth had not had an unhappy life. That was the reality. There'd been sad moments, as there was for everyone, but she had memories that were sweet and would melt in her mouth like chocolate to comfort her on long nights when the dark seemed eternal.

Sure you do. In fact it seemed Elizabeth had nothing but happy memories for such a grimly serious person. So...as the joker would say: Why so serious?

Because you put all the bad feelings into her.

"Never loses her temper." "Such a sweet woman." "So quiet."

All words and phrases used to describe her. Except...that hadn't always been true, had it? She'd been a *loud* child. And she'd surely had a temper; she used to unintentionally scare the other kids though she never meant to. She was just bossy and very sure of herself. All traits that disappeared later.

And then popped up in Liz.

"I'm scared," Liz whispered finally. They were both lying on the bed, facing each other in the dark. The lights had been turned off hours ago. It seemed as if it had been ages. It was too dark for the women to see each other, but each could feel the breath of the other against her face.

"Me too," Elizabeth admitted.

"What do you think that guy wanted from us?"

To integrate us and then use us for the Subset. Because split like this, we're a loose cannon. But whole, and with our powers unfettered...I don't think they have anything or anyone quite like us.

She was quiet, though. She was the one after all who read (as there could only be one with a certain definable trait; it was all beginning to seem obvious) and so on this subject she was ahead of Liz. Not for long. How long would it take Liz to fish out the information from her mind? Maybe only long enough for her to fall asleep. And then Liz would share her dreams and fears and perhaps see that there could only be one future for them and that was no future.

Because Elizabeth *was* willing to integrate. For the simple reason that if she was the dominant personality, she was far less likely to "disappear" than Liz. She viewed it more as swallowing Liz whole. Somehow though she didn't think Liz would like that idea.

Feeling Liz next to her in the dark, knowing that Liz was a creation of hers, an aspect of herself, made everything seem different. She felt closer to Liz and in some odd way a little different than before, not so intimidated. This was part of her. She needed to accept all of herself, even the parts she had once cast off. Her rage, her loudness, her femininity, her sexuality. So when Liz leaned in and lightly kissed her lips, Elizabeth didn't pull back. Liz had very soft lips, and her kiss was surprisingly gentle. Elizabeth responded, kissing her back just as gently, slowly rubbing her hand in circles over Liz's narrow back. Over the sweatshirt, then under it to the warm little furnace of that body, the delicate back with the slight protrusions of bird-like bones just under the flesh. She lightly brushed her lips down, kissing Liz's neck.

Liz shifted, her own embrace becoming rougher, moving her head to nibble and then bite at Elizabeth's neck. This should have bothered Elizabeth, but she had some dim memory of long ago, in adolescence perhaps, being far more aggressive sexually than she later was and having a special fondness for biting. Neck, breasts, all of it so delicious that how could one resist? Women were beautiful, and when Elizabeth hit puberty, she'd realized just how much she felt this to be true. She wanted Liz to devour her whole; and then she wanted to devour Liz whole. All so sweet like strawberries and cream. They did not touch below the waist, at least not under the clothes. Just gentle rubbing. There was time for more later.

And everything…everything brought them closer. Physically, mentally, emotionally. Elizabeth could not fear Liz anymore. If what Mr. Todd had said was true, she needed to embrace Liz in every sense of the word. And didn't some cold calculating part of Elizabeth's mind count on that, want it, eager to see what it would lead to?

For I will devour her in the end.

She smiled in the darkness.

And it was good that Liz could not see that smile for there were a great many teeth suddenly visible.

* * *

Liz knew that she was at a disadvantage but she could not explain how or why. She had Elizabeth's arms wrapped around her, but instead of feeling safe, she felt smothered. It seemed as if Elizabeth could crush her like a python. Even worse was the feeling that if she were capable, Elizabeth *would* do it.

Why?

Because she doesn't like herself.

Wasn't there always a fine line with Elizabeth? That phenomenal self-control…in her drinking…the way she'd quit smoking years before…everything rigidly self-controlled and to what purpose? Why, to keep her alive of course. Because every impulse in her cried out for self-destruction. Deep down,

Elizabeth craved death. And here…here was the golden chance for her to self-destruct without actually having to commit suicide. Suicide, that hissing snake-like word. No. Just obliterate good ole Liz, and you'd have a new and improved Elizabeth… and no more Liz.

Elizabeth might be liking that idea.

Liz chewed it over and thought it had an especially lousy taste. Unlike Elizabeth, she *did* want to live. She was the fighter. So why should she get obliterated for a creature like Elizabeth who did not even want to live?

Now that she'd thought it over very carefully, she decided she shouldn't. Hell, Elizabeth couldn't integrate her without her consent (at least Liz hoped she couldn't, but she really couldn't be sure, could she?) Liz didn't know how this integration thing would work, but she was determined to fight it every step of the way.

She bit Elizabeth's neck lightly then harder and felt Elizabeth's breathing getting more rapid.

Oh yes. I have your number. And I will make myself indispensable to you. I'll make you…love me.

She pulled back a little and stroked Elizabeth's hair tenderly. How springy it felt now that it was short! "Tell me what you want," she whispered.

Want? Elizabeth didn't know whether Liz meant from her, from life or just in terms of physical affection.

"I want to trust you," she admitted honestly.

Liz was quiet, not sure how to take that. It had not been said in a cruel way. On the contrary, it was if Liz had asked such a direct question that it had surprised the truth out of Elizabeth.

"How can I make that happen?" she asked.

Stop taking delight in murder.

But she could hardly blame Liz for that, could she? If Liz was a split off from herself, the desire to murder had come from her, Elizabeth. So where had it come from in her? She hadn't been born that way.

It's not a desire to murder; it's a desire for revenge. But you'll keep killing because nothing satisfies. You aren't getting revenge against the ones you really need to find.

She felt her eyes welling up with tears. God damn it. God fucking damn it. She didn't need this right now. She wiped at her eyes with her free hand. Her other hand was still chained to Liz.

"I was raped," she said aloud in the darkness. Her mouth trembled. She wanted to flay her own flesh off, just to get rid of the memory.

Liz reached over and embraced her. Elizabeth buried her head against her shoulder.

She'd said it aloud. Finally. If only to herself. Elizabeth cried. Liz did not. She'd known about the rape. Not the details, but she didn't need the details. She'd known. It was *Elizabeth* who hadn't known, who'd needed to hear it said aloud, if only to face the truth for herself. She let Elizabeth cry for a while, tears that were long overdue, and finally Elizabeth stopped and just lay silently against Liz's shoulder. Liz could feel that some of the ever-present rigidity and tension had left her body. She waited until she sensed that Elizabeth was calm again or at least as calm as she could get.

"What would you like to do about it?" she asked.

"Kill them," Elizabeth said. There was no hesitation in her voice. It was very hard and very decisive.

"So let's do it."

"I can't!" Now there was the frustration, the frustration Elizabeth had carried for years. "I don't know their names. I don't even know what they look like. It was dark, and their faces...when I was seven I was hit by a car, it made it so it's hard for me to recognize faces...It's why I hate groups, but I wouldn't recognize them if I saw them again. I know it. That's why I never—I never called the police. Or told anyone."

"I wasn't hit by a car," Liz said calmly.

"So?"

Sulky. Elizabeth didn't understand the point yet.

"So I don't have your problem with faces. And the memory is in you still which means you can share it with me—make me relive it with you. *I'll* know their faces. If they're out there...

let's do your thing. Your Controlled Remote Viewing. We'll find them."

Elizabeth had stopped breathing. Now she exhaled slowly. "Do you think—do you think it would work?"

Liz shrugged. "Why wouldn't it?"

"All right." Elizabeth took a deep shuddering breath. "Then let's do this."

She touched her forehead against Liz's, and they lay there like that. Then…Elizabeth relived the rape in her mind, as much detail as she could remember and that was a lot, and Liz relived it with her. When it was done, they both pulled back from each other and simply sat in silence for a long time.

"Damn. I'm sorry," Liz said finally.

"Thank you."

It had been bad. A lot worse than Liz had imagined, and she'd dealt with some pretty heavy shit of her own, but that didn't mean that it made it any easier to see someone else go through it and to feel and experience it all. Mostly the helplessness was the worst. The feeling of being powerless and simply not-good-enough to defend yourself.

"We'll find them," Liz whispered.

Elizabeth's face was wet, but in the dark, she smiled. She and Liz put their heads together and began whispering silently, so silently that even the hidden microphones throughout the room could not pick out what they were saying.

They hatched dark plans, and those plans tasted sweet.

* * *

"So much for Byron Todd," Peters said, as he watched the two women curled up in the dark on the bed together through the infrared camera. He rubbed the mole on the side of his nose a bit more vigorously, but otherwise did not seem very concerned.

"Yes, well…" Paul shrugged, not sitting down, just folding his arms as he also observed the camera and the women on it.

"He always was an arrogant fuck. Gave me the creeps if you want to know the truth, and that's not an easy thing to make happen in this business."

"This rape business. How do you propose we deal with it?" Peters asked, ceasing to rub his mole, turning away from the camera and swiveling around in his chair.

Paul made a face and shifted slightly. "I say we give her what she wants. Let her get her revenge. I think when she has, she and Liz will merge and then...then we can work with her on what *we* need done."

"Do you think she's stable enough? Seems like a lot of work for one neurotic woman." Peters tone, though, suggested real concern rather than outright dismissal.

Paul was quiet for some moments, then finally sat down in the swivel chair adjacent to Peters that also faced the viewing room. "She's better than our best and that's been with her working at about ten percent of her capacity. This woman isn't just psychic—she literally shapes reality, wills things into or out of existence. If we had anyone else who could even *begin* to do what she does, we wouldn't waste our time. But we don't. And if we can harness her...there's no limit to what we can do."

"But how cooperative will she be?"

Paul shifted and smiled a little. "If we help her find the men who raped her...I would say very cooperative. That rape is her Achilles' heel. Hell, are you sure you didn't send the men to rape her in the first place?"

Peters just laughed. And then laughed some more.

* * *

Concentrate. On every detail of the most horrible event of your life. Concentrate until everything comes into sharp focus. Maybe you can't remember the whole of the face, but you can remember the shape of the mouth. Concentrate on that. The small tattoo between the webbing of the thumb and the forefinger on one. The particular smell of the other. Concentrate on everything...and then focus. Focus on where are they now. You know the odds are good they are in prison or dead, such is what happens to this type of lowlife, and time has a way of working its own revenge, but for once, you do not want time working revenge; that honor is reserved for you.

And you're in luck. They're still in New York. Scumbags like that never leave. What would they do? Retire to the country? At this, Elizabeth smiled bitterly. Focus some more. Now she can see the room where one of them is holed up. Ratty tenement, occupants heavy into drugs. The other one fared better, bastard actually has a reasonably decent place and is that…yes, a live-in girlfriend, maybe even a wife but animals like that never get married, everyone knows that, so it's likely his latest fuck-buddy. Well, hopefully they're done because he won't be fucking for long.

The Subset had come to them, taken her away from Liz and promised their help…transportation, money, help from similarly gifted people, all of it, if Elizabeth would agree to work for them for the period of one year on a special mission afterward. There was to be no disobedience, no questioning of orders. It was all or nothing.

Her mouth was dry, and she craved whiskey. The offer was a no-brainer. She signed every paper they put in front of her as fast as they could pull them out of the binders. It was worth it. She even found herself craving a cigarette.

She and Liz talked. They talked and talked. The barrier that had separated them on the subject of killing no longer existed. In fact, it was Elizabeth who came up with the most gruesome of plans, torments that made Liz's skinning alive look like child's play.

She and Liz often held hands, and sometimes it seemed that Liz's hands were fading away and Elizabeth could only see her own hand, empty and holding nothing. This usually happened when they were discussing the torture, what they'd do when they found Elizabeth's rapists. Elizabeth had put all of her anger into Liz. Now…now she was reclaiming it, and it felt good. Because goddamn it, she had a *right* to be angry. For no reason other than the fact that she'd been born female, she'd been tortured and raped for a night by perfect strangers. She'd been unable to stand up for herself and not for lack of trying. But her punches had gone wild, bounced off the men like marshmallows, and then her hands had simply been pinned, and she'd been unable to do anything. Helpless. And all the boxing lessons and handgun lessons in the world later couldn't undo that. It was a cliché case of locking the barn door after the horse was gone. There was, she knew, only one way to reclaim her life, and that was to do to them what had been done to her.

Liz will disappear.

Except she knew better now. Liz would not disappear; Liz would simply become a part of her as she must have once been. They'd be one person, but twice as strong as either of them was now.

"Are you at ease with this?" Elizabeth asked, referring to the situation.

"No," Liz admitted. "But…I'm willing to see what happens."

She was still vacillating. Sometimes she saw it as Elizabeth saw it…the ultimate closeness between them, a way to be stronger and together forever. Other times…she simply saw it as disappearing, being obliterated.

She wanted to help Elizabeth fight back against her attackers, but she didn't want to sacrifice herself for it either. She decided she'd go along to New York with Elizabeth and help her as long as it felt comfortable and then…then she'd decide what to do if it looked like integration was going to occur.

The remote viewing and tracking process took exactly one week. It was an emotional time for both women. Elizabeth was forced to relive memories she'd worked very hard to bury, and Liz was constantly contemplating the thought of her own extinction (or possible evolution if she could persuade herself to take the high road). At night they cuddled.

This is an extension of myself, Elizabeth thought. She's not even real. But in her arms, Liz felt very real. Embracing Liz, feeling her heat within her arms, was like hugging herself and there was something so terribly awkward about it that Elizabeth longed to be holding any other woman in the world in her arms.

Someone whose skin was not so hot, so lit from within, a woman separate from Elizabeth with her own dreams and nightmares. That would have to come later. For now, she needed to nurture this part of herself and that did not come naturally. Feeling Liz squirming against her one night, Elizabeth was struck by a wave of revulsion for this angry destructive part of herself and pushed Liz away as hard as she could. Liz kicked back at her in the darkness, and Elizabeth reached out reflexively, smacking her hard across the face without really thinking about it. There was a loud cracking sound, the flesh was very firm under her hand, and it felt good. Elizabeth thought she might like to do it again, and then she felt a wave of shame wash over her. She'd never hit another person unless it had been in self-defense, and this clearly wasn't. She heard Liz's sharp intake of breath and felt the woman shifting on the bed as she sat up.

"Why did you do that?" Liz whispered softly.

Because I don't like you, Elizabeth thought silently. But that wasn't fair. She did not dislike Liz. It was a part of herself she was wrestling with, and thus, by extension, Liz. Owning her anger, but focusing it was very hard.

You'll have to do better than this, she thought in the dark, if you're going to confront the rapists.

"I'm sorry," she whispered aloud, and she *was* sorry suddenly, for the needless violence, the harshness and cruelty she'd inflicted, not upon Liz, but upon herself for all these years, and she held out her arms to embrace Liz, and even as she did, she could feel that she was embracing a part of herself.

Everything had been leading up to this. Liz's killing of rapists and pedophiles. Repeating the same action over and over again, gaining temporary satisfaction, but no peace, because she was killing the wrong men. She was living out what Elizabeth needed, but going about it all wrong. As for Liz, she sat quietly in the dark, her cheek stinging, and knew that her days were numbered. Elizabeth was wrestling with something, and Liz could not relate. She wrestled with nothing. For her, the past was concrete and irrelevant, and her actions were as necessary and inevitable as the sun. There was no growth, no change, just an unyielding force of nature, stuck in an infinite loop that replayed over and over, long after the tune had grown warped and the record scratched.

Make her love you.

Something told Liz this was her only key to survival and important for many reasons. But she really didn't know how to go about it. She had no blueprint of her own emotions. It was not love Elizabeth wanted, and nothing so crass as money or fame or that sort of thing. But nonetheless, she knew Elizabeth wanted something if only for the simple reason that people who truly want nothing don't bother living for very long. Elizabeth wasn't very firmly tethered to life, but she was still here which meant she wanted *something* no matter how nebulous.

Liz shared Elizabeth's memories at night, their heads pressed close together. Liz shared all her fears; Elizabeth shared her indifference to danger. Liz shared her promiscuity with both genders; Elizabeth shared her celibacy since Darcy. Darcy seemed to reveal something about Elizabeth, and Liz chewed over that connection like a dog with a bone, trying to figure out what it was. It was not love though certainly there had been love between the two women and a strong friendship, but what had created it was…understanding.

Darcy had understood Elizabeth. Upon understanding her, she had also liked Elizabeth and cared for her very much which was an added bonus and good for Elizabeth's self-esteem, which hadn't been high on the best of days back then. But even if Darcy had despised Elizabeth, Liz suspected Elizabeth still would have been enamored of Darcy simply because the woman understood her. Elizabeth did not understand herself very well, and thus she craved understanding from others, someone who could see and accept her. Once Liz was aware of this, she realized that now *she* understood Elizabeth, and would Elizabeth really give this up in exchange for being alone again…albeit with an understanding of herself, assuming they integrated?

It was hard to say. But, armed with her knowledge, Liz snuggled with Elizabeth, kissed her often, and listened to her constantly. Her survival depended upon love.

What survival?

Perhaps survival also depended upon evolution. Liz knew she was not educated, but felt she was quick and clever and felt certain things deeply and instinctively. She could feel that things were shifting within Elizabeth, deep things, monsters awakening that had been sleeping for many years. In contrast, she felt empty inside, watching through plate glass as these changes happened while she stayed the same, a child stranded in the road as the car receded into the distance, growing smaller and smaller, leaving her behind.

Don't leave me.

And some part of her understood that Elizabeth would not leave her, could not leave her, but staying with Elizabeth might mean changing. Becoming something else. And that was tied in with love, for love changes people too, and this was a love story, albeit a very different type.

Love of self so that I may love another.

Did the thought belong to Elizabeth or Liz? It seemed to belong to them both. They breathed it simultaneously, face to face in the night, staring into one another's eyes, searching for answers and a sense of connection. Smack her, abuse her, connect to her, cry with her…in the end, Liz was chained to Elizabeth, without need of handcuffs, and as the week passed, they grew accepting of this situation. Neither could understand herself without first understanding the other, and intuitively they knew this. Now it was only a matter of embracing everything, the darkness as well as the light, for Elizabeth to move forward.

Sunday: time to go. The door to the tiny room slid open. Elizabeth and Liz were curled up on the bed, holding hands, a frown on one face, faint smile on the other, much like the masques of comedy and tragedy. A man stepped in warily. These women had a reputation, and he was only a career man with low rank, designed to fetch them for the final adventure, but he'd heard of them and knew how dangerous they could be. The overhead fluorescent light was on, but the women had been up late whispering, Elizabeth sharing secrets with herself for the first time in years, and they slept on. The man paused, studying

the blond and brunette heads, so close together and it struck
him how they were sleeping in a yin and yang formation, each
completing the other, forming a perfect circle.

He cleared his throat then spoke. "Time to go."

Two pairs of eyes opened and blinked simultaneously. The
women yawned and sat up, adept by now at moving in rhythm.

"We're free," Liz said smiling and stretching luxuriantly.

Elizabeth smiled back gently. Not yet, she thought. But
soon…soon maybe we'll *really* be free. I'll be free.

And it was a very odd feeling to stare at Liz and wonder if
the thing she was being freed from was herself.

* * *

Return to New York. The place where the nightmares
began. They flew in on a red-eye flight, the two women, dressed
in pantsuits provided by the Subset, sitting side by side on the
plane. Liz was pale and unusually subdued, her fingers twisting
in her lap. Two men from the Subset sat discreetly behind them.
Liz did not look good, but Elizabeth looked even worse. Her
eyes were shadowed and dark, her face grim. Inside her mind,
everything was shades of gray fading into black. What she
wanted was to reclaim herself. The need was pulsing in her like
a heartbeat.

At four in the morning, the plane landed, the wheels
thumping gently against the tarmac. Around them, seeming
to be far away and coming from a great distance, people were
talking. Only Liz and Elizabeth and the Subset were quiet. None
of them had any need for words. They left the plane, making
their way rapidly through the airport. There was no need to
stop at baggage claim as none of them had brought any bags.
This was going to be a quick trip.

I wonder what comes after? a small part of Elizabeth's mind
asked. It was a good question. Born in blood, perhaps life would
come after. Healing. Maybe even love. Not just the love of self
which Elizabeth was late on discovering, but the love that can
come after, the love of seeing another person fully as you have
finally been seen, even if it is just by yourself at the beginning.

The air outside was moist, putting down a layer that felt like a damp blanket against the skin. Elizabeth tilted her face up momentarily to a gray sky and let it soothe her, then a hand gently took her arm and guided her over to a waiting Town Car. Liz followed, her eyes focused on the ground, gray unyielding concrete but full of cracks. She no longer felt relevant. The best of her was being sapped away.

The car wound through the streets, flanked on every side by traffic. A world in motion, but inside the protective bubble of the Subset car, everything was very still and very quiet, a heart waiting to take its next beat but not quite ready yet.

They drove to Brooklyn and the car eased to a stop at the curb of a small brown inconspicuous two-story town home. Elizabeth looked out the window.

That's it.

Behind those walls was a man who'd haunted her nightmares for years. The place he lived seemed so small and insignificant in daylight, not larger than life at all but bite-size. She could feel him inside. Was he the monster or had he made her the monster? Maybe it was monsters all the way down. She got out of the car and walked up to the door, Liz following silently. The car waited behind them, faceless and blank, no judgment there, just an empty vessel. The front door opened. It might have been locked when they arrived but before Elizabeth's need, all doors opened. Down the hallways, wooden floors, a musty odor in the air. Outside the blackness beginning to ease, backing away in the face of the oncoming morning light. It would be night for just a little while longer.

Into the apartment then into the bedroom.

There he is. Sleeping in bed, comfortable, sleeping with a surety and peace that Elizabeth hadn't felt for years. No gun beside that bed. Her hand reached out and found Liz's beside her, no longer burning hot but still solid enough, comforting her.

Liz expected Elizabeth to act and back off. To make the kill clean and quick. Elizabeth didn't. Why on earth should she? Her hand tightened on Liz's.

They stood in the bedroom door of the apartment of the man who'd raped and sodomized Elizabeth, and Elizabeth wanted nothing more than to make him feel what she had felt. Helpless. Her emotion was all-consuming, draining everything around her.

Liz felt herself flickering in and out of existence. She could not control it. Elizabeth was taking away all her anger and hatred and expelling it all outward onto the source of it, and Liz had been a creature fueled by rage. She had so little else. The rapist couldn't scream because someone had shoved his own underwear into his mouth. That was the only time Elizabeth ever spoke.

"Remember me?" she whispered as she ripped his underwear off and rammed it hard into his mouth, knocking out both front teeth. All this she did without moving, using her mind, and she could see the fear in his dark eyes as they bored into hers and worst of all, she saw the vague memory of her rape in his mind, but it was just that…vague. It had not meant to him what it had meant to her. And that infuriated her the most. She had been just another bitch to him, not the first rape and not the last. Just a bit of extra fun on a robbery.

And there was something else, something about someone tipping him off to her place specifically but that vision was gray and not visible, hidden behind the veil.

No matter. Elizabeth slashed and tore and every bit of terror he felt took away some of her own rage. She was giving it back, all the emotions she should never have had to feel in the first place.

Elizabeth bit her lip, smashing his head repeatedly against the wall, tearing off limbs, and biting with invisible teeth… biting and ripping and tearing. Arteries spurted, blood flew… The police officer who would enter the scene a few hours later, a veteran officer of twenty-three years, would throw up. There was blood and flesh everywhere, blood oozing down the walls, dripping from the ceiling, soaking into the carpet in puddles.

Liz tried to scream, but she had no voice left. She closed her eyes at some point, but her head was still filled with blood. She,

who'd shed so much blood in her life, but she'd only shared half
the rage of Elizabeth—now, together, their full fury was being
felt, and it terrified her.

I don't want it, Liz thought.

But it was far too late for that. Elizabeth wanted it, and what
Elizabeth wanted, Elizabeth got.

Tiefe Wassers sind nicht still.

Where had that come from? Liz spoke no foreign languages.
But of course Elizabeth did. She spoke five, including English,
compliments of her time in the military with the Subset: German,
Spanish, Russian, and a smattering of Urdu. It was Elizabeth's
thought that Liz had picked up for they were merging and the
German translated into: *Deep waters don't run still.* A little play on
words, Elizabeth liked that, and German lent itself well to word
play and puns, the logical structure and the dark rich sound of
the language appealing to the Slavic nature of Elizabeth's blood.
Only Russian surpassed German in her love of language. Liz
remembered reading (or was it Elizabeth who had read it? No
matter now, the lines between them were growing dimmer and
dimmer) that in 1942 as the Russians advanced into Germany,
some of them slit the throats of their prisoners and drank hot
German blood from a boot. Blood running down the throat,
warm and rich and thick, after a winter spent freezing and
dining on cold German corpses. Yes, Elizabeth had her heritage
all right. The Russian military once trained with three bullets a
year because they had no money for more. Yet they were still the
fiercest military force in the world because they simply didn't
give up. It was not in their nature. The Russians were a poor
people and often an unlucky people, but most of all, they were
a determined people.

Elizabeth laughed and laughed. And soon Liz laughed with
her, consumed by Elizabeth, and when at last the murder was
done, Elizabeth was no longer clean, but drenched in warm
blood, only the whites of her eyes showing, and she knew this
blood was on her hands forever, but what she had not counted
on was how warm it felt. She licked her lips and tasted the slight

coppery taste of fresh blood, and the taste was sweet and sweeter now than any love she'd ever known.

The remnants of what had once been a man or at least a homo sapien were strewn about the apartment.

When it was done, everything was layered red upon red. Liz had grown very pale and clammy, feeling as if she might faint any moment. She was still holding Elizabeth's hand, but she could no longer feel that hand.

"Elizabeth?" she whispered.

"Shut up. We have work to do."

Elizabeth's eyes were fixed on the blood streaming down the walls. She imagined that she could taste it in her mouth and it melted on her tongue like a magical elixir. She had never felt so strong, so whole or so alive. At least not since she had been raped, first physically by this fucking animal and then later, mentally by the Subset.

Today the bill comes due. Everybody pays. House wins.

She laughed. Liz closed her eyes because it was horrible laugh, menacing and yet not insane. The perfect sanity and total lack of humor in that laugh were what made it so chilling.

They moved out the door, Liz barely aware of where they were going. Back into the hallway with the gray carpet and the smell of boiled cabbage in the air. And just below the smell, a sick sweet meaty smell emanating from Apartment 213 where Elizabeth had taken care of old business.

Half the job done. Now on to the other half.

She tugged at Liz's hand. Liz didn't move. Elizabeth stopped and looked back, noticing for the first time how sickly and transparent Liz looked. An expression of annoyance crossed her face.

"What is it?" she snapped irritably.

"I love you," Liz whispered, her eyes pleading.

Something flickered behind Elizabeth's eyes then or maybe that was only wishful thinking on Liz's part.

"I love you too," Elizabeth said. "But it's not really enough, is it?"

No. There was nothing to say to that. It simply wasn't enough. There could be no love with an incomplete person. In order to love, Elizabeth first had to reclaim herself, anger and all. Liz closed her eyes in resignation then opened them and followed Elizabeth down the hallway and back outside to the deserted early morning street and the waiting car. They were on to do the next job.

In the car, Liz leaned her head on Elizabeth's shoulder. Though she'd physically done nothing, she was very tired and even through the fabric of Elizabeth's shirt, Liz could feel the heat emanating from the woman. Elizabeth was on fire inside, burning with her need.

Through more streets, a journey that seemed to take no time at all. Blood drying on Elizabeth's clothes, fading from red to brown. So many things could have gone wrong, but they hadn't. All of this was meant to be.

There were no pedestrians when Liz and Elizabeth reached the next apartment and no one saw them. Elizabeth followed the scent of darkness that was in the building, letting it speak to the darkness within her, carrying it like a package before her.

Return to sender.

It was long overdue but that was all right. Better late than never.

She put her hand on the doorknob outside the apartment. It was gold-colored and greasy, almost warm to the touch. She twisted and it opened, and they both stepped inside. The apartment was small and dingy, faded green carpet on the floor, and a kitchen off to the side. A tall, balding, potbellied man came out of the kitchen carrying a cup of coffee, wearing dirty boxers and a white tanktop. His mouth opened slightly when he saw Elizabeth. Did he see Liz behind her? It was hard to tell. Everything was Elizabeth now.

"Who the fuck are you?" he demanded.

"Someone trying to put things right," Elizabeth said.

There would be more to that to do later. She could already tell. Revenge was not healing. Healing would begin later. This was not the end of her journey but the beginning. The taking back of her power, even if it was only within her own mind. Something she needed to do.

She stared into the eyes of the man who'd done this to her. They were brown but empty, no recognition and nothing behind them for Elizabeth to relate to. She wondered what her own eyes looked like right now. The image of the man doubled in her vision, and Elizabeth blinked, clearing her vision, feeling a small trickle of warmth as a single bit of wetness kissed one cheek. What was she feeling? The box was open, and it was all coming out now, too many emotions to name and identify, emotions that had been stolen away and hidden in the attic for all these years.

"You stole me," she said, her voice cracking. And the words were strange and the syntax stranger, but wasn't it the truth, the truest thing she could have said? It wasn't just rape, a penis entering a vagina. This man had stolen her from herself, taking away her sense of safety and trust in her own body, her connection to herself. "I want it back," Elizabeth said, and there was so much that "it" encompassed. Everything she'd lost, and she could not undo the past, but she could make peace with it on her own terms and go forward so that tomorrow would not have to be the same as today.

Why did they always say women have no right to be angry? For her whole life, it seemed she had been hearing that in one form or another, even before the rape. Her temper had been rebuked as a child. Women were supposed to forgive and accept. *Why?* What was healthy about that? Turn the other cheek and you only end up with red cheeks and a smothered scream within, biting your fist in the night to keep it from spilling out. Sometimes anger is justified. Own it, wear it, taste it, dance with it. It tastes like black licorice and fits like a suit that is snug but tailor-made. *This is not who I am, but it is part of me. And I own all of it.*

"You're fucking crazy," the man sneered. "Stupid bitch, get the hell out of here."

"I'm not crazy," Elizabeth said, and in her bones she felt the truth of that statement. Damaged, yes, but not incapable of healing, not incapable of moving forward. She turned and looked at Liz. Those eyes were confused, and Elizabeth saw the futility there, the way it all dead-ended. There could be no moving forward for Liz. She was a dead-end child, ruled by her rage.

Is that what you shall become?

Elizabeth would not be ruled by her rage. Owning it was not the same as being consumed by it, and for the first time, Elizabeth felt the rage taking a shape, something small and square that could be contained within her and addressed without being all-consuming.

I can evolve, she thought, staring at Liz who was all her anger personified. She can't. And what Elizabeth felt was not anger but tenderness, a desire to wrap Liz and all her rage in a package with pretty ribbons and bows and protect it. She put her arm around the other woman's shoulders. Liz flinched from the touch. She didn't know about rage that wasn't all-consuming.

This doesn't make it right. But it makes it into something I can live with and move beyond.

That was enough. It would have to be. Sometimes good enough is just what you need. Elizabeth did not need to go back to the woman she was before she was raped; she just needed to be a complete woman.

The man reached for her. Elizabeth stretched her mind and snapped his wrist, breaking it in one smooth fluid motion. He screamed.

"Hurts, doesn't it?" Elizabeth asked. But unlike the first man, there was no satisfaction in this. It was what needed to be done, no more and no less. Elizabeth's sense of well-being no longer depended upon this man, his existence or his extinction. She would take him out to protect other women, but her sense of self was no longer contingent upon it.

The man was staring at her, holding his wrist, hopping side to side on his bare feet from the pain. His lips were drawn back, teeth bared. "What the fuck are you?" he hissed.

"A human being," Elizabeth answered simply.

Wasn't that always what she'd been and wanted to be seen as? Just a human being with the same rights as anyone and the same needs. Not a creature to be used or abused at the whims of another.

"Bitch." The man lunged at her.

Elizabeth smacked him back, and he fell on the floor, legs sprawling, landing on his backside.

She did this without touching him, and his eyes widened in fear. Elizabeth took a step toward him, and he tried to scramble backward, using his good hand.

"Fear is a terrible thing," Elizabeth intoned, and her eyes were far away even as they looked at him. A thousand-yard stare there, eyes staring into blackness and they had been staring long enough to see the things that move within that darkness.

Elizabeth wanted to ask "Why?" but it was a senseless question. There was no reason. He'd done it because he could and perhaps he'd been hired or perhaps not, but in the end, he had enjoyed what he did and that had been enough. There are no reasons sometimes for the worst things, and that was a truth Elizabeth could accept and live with. She would make her own sense from all this. Patterns are in everything, but they are only what the mind sees, its innate need to impose order onto chaos. Which is the real truth? There is none, only what the eye allows itself to see.

Elizabeth killed him quickly. She did not do it from mercy. She did it because there was no need to do otherwise. She'd expunged her rage on the first man. Now she was just tired and ready to move forward with the rest of her life.

Inside, she felt a small flame burning, a focal point. A center. She had not felt centered and focused for a long time. *I take everything into myself.*

Liz was gone. Drawn back into the mind from whence she'd came.

One killer and one...whatever Elizabeth was now.

She had no name for herself.

But whatever she was, she was whole. A blank slate. *Tabula rasa*. She would go from here.

She walked out into the hallway, not caring who saw her. Everything now was just as it should be, and she could deal with anything life brought her way.

"Mr. Elizabeth?"

Two men in gray suits were waiting for her. And these men had seen and done a great many horrific things in their long and strange lives, but even they paled before Elizabeth covered in blood. "Are you…finished?"

Elizabeth smiled and showed her teeth. Her many, many teeth and the men flinched back.

"Quite," Elizabeth said.

One of the men stepped forward tremulously and draped a blanket over her shoulders to hide the blood. It didn't cover nearly all of it. There was simply too much.

"The car is waiting downstairs," he said.

Elizabeth nodded. The Subset had delivered her rapists to her, or rather delivered her to her rapists, but they had given her what she wanted. The rest was up to her.

For now she would give them what they wanted.

"Let's go," she said.

And later, she thought, maybe later…she would give them what they deserved.

She looked up and laughed again. The two men on either side of her were well-trained to show no emotion, but inside, both of them shuddered.

They walked in silence to the waiting car.

For more Spinsters Ink titles please visit:

www.BellaBooks.com

Bella Books and Distribution
P.O. Box 10543
Tallahassee, FL 32302

Phone: 800-729-4992